Breathe Again

DAN RING

Blue Mountain Publishing

624 S. 12th Street

Paragould, AR 72450

Breathe Again is fiction. Any similarity between characters in the book, excluding immediate family members of the author, and real persons is unintentional and purely coincidential. Names, characters, places, and incidents, while based on actual events, have been altered and used ficticiously.

CONTENTS

DEDICATION

When you lose someone you love, part of you dies. This book is dedicated to those pieces of me that died, and yet breathe again.

My dad, Sherman Ring, born April 2, 1934; died October 20, 1998. He did not teach me how to live with many words. He simply lived and let me watch.

My wife, Debbie Ring, born August 8, 1957; died January 18, 2007. If God is love, then true love never dies. For I am convinced that neither the grave nor life, neither angels nor principalities, neither the present nor the future, nor any powers, neither height nor depth, nor anything else in all creation, will be able to separate us from the love of God that is in Christ Jesus our Lord.

My son, Jason Ring, born September 11, 1979; died August 3, 2013. He could tell a story better than me.

When Debbie was sick, early of the morning, we would walk through the neighborhood as the sun was rising. I would hold her hand, and say, "Close your eyes baby. Breathe. Just breathe and believe. Believe that God is holding your hand and guiding ever step you take. Believe the gentle breeze caressing your face is the very breath of God. Believe that with every breath you take, God is preparing you for Kingdom work. Believe that God will use your story to touch many lives."

As we walked, I didn't see it coming. God was preparing her for His Kingdom. He was preparing me for Kingdom work. I would be the one to tell her story. I would be the one to give God glory. This is her story, and I am convinced that it will indeed touch many lives.

PROLOGUE

He rode the wind like a majestic stallion, wild and free. He could not tame her. Her love was as fierce as a raging fire, racing to the water's edge where it must die. With her smile, she took his breath away. The child of perdition, dancing with a fallen limb, in the dark of night, took his son from him.

Most men spend their lives chasing dreams they'll never catch. For the lucky few, who grasp the wind, to place it in a bottle, constrained by the shackles of their own choosing, they must watch it die, and never know its scent again.

This is the story of a man with nothing left to lose. Love and loss scattered by the winds of adversity, like dandelions in the early spring. Before the beauty of a flower can be seen, a seed must fall to the ground and die.

I chased the wind, I questioned God, demanding answers. In the end, I learned that a man must die before he ever lives.

1

SHE TOOK MY BREATH AWAY

I had been looking forward to this day all week. It was Friday, and that meant, Jaslynn, my granddaughter would be spending the night with me. Her brother, Jax, was going to spend the night with his MeMe. Jennifer, my daughter, had to work late, so it would be just the two of us. I had planned to pick Jaslynn up after school. We would go to the park for a play-date, before picking up pizza and ice cream on the way home. After dinner, we'd pop popcorn and watch a movie. She'd climb up in my lap, and we would read a bedtime story. Sometimes, before we finished the story, I would close the book and ask her to tell me how she thought the story should end. Most times, I liked Jaslynn's ending better. Her creativity, and vivid imagination will no doubt serve her well, if she chases her dream to be an artist or entertainer.

First, I wanted to go by the cemetery and place a rose on Debbie's grave. Today would have been our 40th wedding anniversary. The fragrance of the rose, a sweet aide memoire of the scent of love, a beautiful and fragile thing, but capable of drawing blood when threatened. Absent in the moment, I pricked my finger on a thorn; a drop of love fell to the ground. As I placed the rose on her stone, I noticed a woman walking toward me. I didn't see her when I got out of my car. I didn't notice her as I walked to Debbie's grave. It was like she floated in on a gentle breeze, and there she was. She was walking toward me; and I was overwhelmed by her presence. She looked just like Debbie. It literally took my breath away. I had heard, that when someone you love dies, there will be times when you think you see them at a distance, or you see their face in a crowd. You think you hear their voice, or you smell their perfume. I was not lost in a crowd, straining for something that was out of reach. What I saw was walking right toward me, and I couldn't move. As she got closer, time slowed down. She stopped for a moment, as if to ask if it was okay for her to come closer. As I gazed into her eyes, I could tell that she was holding something back. I was certain that she had something that she wanted to say. I must have said something: I don't know. I don't remember. I do remember the smell of honeysuckle. I remember the cool breeze, and the sun on my face. I remember what she was wearing, the color of her hair, and her ear rings. I remember the way she walked and the way she stood there as she talked.

She said, "Can I ask you something?"

I said, "Sure."

She said, "Does it ever get easier?"

I hesitated for just a moment before I answered. I said, "No. It gets different. But I don't think it ever gets easier."

She said, "My son is buried out here. He died in an automobile accident."

I said, "My son, is buried here also. He died in an automobile accident four years ago. He is buried right here next to my wife. She died ten years ago, and I still miss her." I wanted to say, "She was a beautiful woman, and you look just like her", but I didn't.

I'm captivated by this woman that I had never met before. Yet somehow, there seemed to be a common thread that had drawn us together at that moment, to mend a tear in the fabric of life, on this sacred piece of ground. She asked me something that I'll never forget. It was as if, from the very depth of her soul, she was hoping that I would say yes. She asked me, "Do you ever talk to her?"

No one had ever asked me that question before. No staff member at church, no close friend, no family member, no one had ever dared ask that question before. Without hesitation, and with a tear rolling down my face, I said, "Every night. I tell her every night that I miss her, and that I still love her."

As tears rolled down the face of this angel standing in front of me, biting her lower lip, she nodded her head ever so slightly, and said, "Wow." Everything within me wanted to reach out and wipe her tears away, and hold her close to let her know it was going to be okay. There was something drawing me to her and holding me back at the same time. She just stood there, and so did I, with tears rolling down our faces, and she said it again. She said, "Wow."

After what seemed like an eternity of the two of us standing there weeping, and sharing with one another a sacrosanct intimacy that only lovers could know, I said, "I've got to go. I need to pick my granddaughter up. She is going to spend the night with me tonight." I turned and started toward my car, but something compelled me to stop. I turned back around and said, "I wish my wife could see her, my granddaughter that is, she looks just like her. She has her Nana Debbie's big brown eyes, and she's got her Nana Debbie's smile." Before I turned, and started toward my car again, I said, "Are you going to be okay?"

She shook her head, and said, "I'll be fine." I stood there for a moment. I think she knew that I wanted to say something else. She smiled at me and said, "What?"

I asked, "Would it be okay if I prayed for you?" She began to cry again, and she shook her head, yes. Without hesitating, she reached out to take hold of my hands as I began to pray. As we stood there holding hands and praying, I knew this was not a chance encounter. This was a predestined appointment of divine design. I didn't know what was happening, or why we met, but I knew something out of the ordinary had just occurred.

Once more, I turned to go to my car, and she said, "You loved him very much didn't you? Your son, you loved him very much. I can see it in his stone. I see life and death. The wind is blowing, the waves are crashing against the rocky shore. As the storms of life rage all around, the lighthouse stands as a beacon of hope in the dark of night. Behind the lighthouse, stands the Son of God, with His arms reaching out to rescue those who have lost their way. The light from the lighthouse, is the love of God that penetrates the darkness with a beam of light in the shape of a cross, providing salvation for those who are perishing.

I love the verse; 'The Lord is my light and my salvation; whom shall I fear? The Lord is my solid rock and my strong tower; of whom shall I be afraid?' Psalm 27:1

It fits the image on the stone. It speaks of an unshakeable love that cannot be moved by the storms of this life; a patient, and loving Father, not wanting anyone to perish, but everyone to come to repentance."

And then, as if she knew my son, she said, "For a little while his light shined bright in the dark of night. You will never know this side of heaven the number of lives he has impacted. You may not see him any longer, convinced that the darkness has overcome his light, but he lives on, and his light still shines."

She had spoken to my very soul. I felt naked, yet unashamed; vulnerable, but safe and secure. She had seen what no one else could see. She saw my tears, and so much more. I sat there in my car, feeling as if I had just shared an intimate experience with a stranger in the cemetery. It felt reckless, and scandalous, but somehow righteous at the same time. I didn't want to leave. Looking back, I noticed this woman that I had just met, still standing there, looking at my wife's stone, and my son's stone next to it. I closed my eyes to breathe in deep, and fill my lungs with the scent of this moment. I wanted to engrave this image on the canvas of my mind. Inhaling and exhaling slowly, as I meticulously painted every stroke. If I were offered all the wealth of the world in exchange for this precious work of art, the proposition would be utterly scorned. Like thunder and lightning in a summer storm, feelings that I thought were dead have been resurrected. A pounding rain could not quench the fire that has been ignited.

Without warning, as quickly as the fire erupted, the flames were extinguished by an incoming text message on my phone. My daughter was confirming that I was on my way to pick up Jaslynn. I could not wait to get my granddaughter, but at the same time I could not dismiss what had just happened. I had met a woman who stirred an emotion in my soul that had not been touched in a long time. I didn't ask her name. I may never see her again, but somehow, deep within me, I know she was there and I was there for a reason. We were there at an appointed place and an appointed time. It was as if we had no say in what took place, we were just players acting out our parts in a predetermined course of events. I don't think I will ever forget that woman, or the look on her face as I walked away, and how she seemed to be drawn to my son's grave and my wife's grave as I drove off. Without even realizing it, this encounter with the stranger in the cemetery had me mesmerized. I pulled up at Jaslynn's school with no memory of driving the thirty miles from the cemetery to the school. Before I knew what had happened, Jaslynn was in the front seat of the car buckling her seat belt, and I was still captivated by the strange woman who had entered my garden uninvited.

"Dandy, can we go and get ice cream?"

"You want ice cream right now?" I asked.

"Sure!" She said.

"We will go to get ice cream then, and you can tell me what you did at school today." I drove and she talked non-stop. I'm not sure she even took a breath before we reached the ice cream shop. After a three-scoop hot fudge sundae, with whipped cream, nuts and two cherries on top, we went to the park, to play for a while before supper.

"Dandy, go down the slide with me." I think some of the other kids and one of the mothers were a little surprised to see me climb up the slide and turn around and go down backwards just like Jaslynn did. Not only were they surprised, but a couple of them thought it quite amusing when I slid off the bottom of the slide and landed on my bottom. Jaslynn obviously thought it was funny, she laughed louder than anyone else. After a couple more trips down the slide, once on my stomach, and backwards one more time, hanging from the monkey bars, and spinning round and round on the merry-go-round until I couldn't walk straight, I surrendered, and yielded to the queen of the playground.

Bowing before the queen, and pleading for

mercy, I humbly asked, "My Lady, do you want cheese pizza or pepperoni pizza?"

She said, "You can rise my lord, if we can get a cheese pizza with mushrooms?" Graced to recline at table of the playground queen, I seized the opportunity to retreat and ordered the pizza. We picked it up on our way home. As we were feasting like royalty on pizza and drinking chocolate milk, the food of Gods and mortal men, she says, "Tell me about Nana Debbie, Dandy."

I imagine that time stood still for a moment, as the angels in heaven witnessed me smile like I had not smiled in a very long time. To hear my granddaughter, say, "I love you, Dandy", is a treasure of infinite value. But, for her to ask me to tell her about her Nana Debbie, nothing could thrill me more. After we finished eating, I cleared the table and said, "Come with me, we will look at some pictures and I will tell you all about Nana Debbie." Jaslynn grabbed my phone. I said, "We won't need my phone."

"But how will we look at pictures without your phone?"

"Before everybody took pictures on their phone, we used to take pictures with a camera. Come into my room. I want to show you something." I pulled a plastic storage container from under my bed. It was full of old photographs. Photographs of me and Nana Debbie when we were young. Photographs of

Jaslynn's mom and her uncle Adam and her uncle Jason, who died in an auto accident when Jaslynn was just two years old. Photographs of my parents, Debbie's parents and her family. Then I got another box out of the closet. It was full of photo albums from a time that seems so long ago. Finally, I picked up our wedding album, I told Jaslynn to come and sit in my lap. I said, "Forty years ago today, Nana Debbie and I got married. These are some pictures that were taken on that day."

"Wow, Nana Debbie was pretty, wasn't she?"

"She was beautiful, just like you. You get your big brown eyes and your beautiful smile from your Nana Debbie. I know, that if she could, she would love to be here with us now. I can see her hugging your neck, and smiling; singing goofy little songs and dancing barefoot in the grass with you."

"Wow, her dress was so beautiful. Do you still love her Dandy?"

"I still love her very much, and I always will. And I miss her very much. I remember the day these pictures were taken like it was yesterday. I remember the day I first met Nana Debbie. I didn't know her name, but I remember the first time she smiled at me, it took my breath away. I went by the grocery store that I used to work at my senior year in high school. I was telling my friend, Sammy, about this girl that I had seen on the road every day for the last month. Sammy and I used to work at the store together. Sammy still worked there, but I had quit several months earlier and started a new job at the shoe factory. It wasn't until my parents moved, that I began seeing this beautiful young girl on my way home from work every day. She would be driving in one direction, and I was driving in the other direction. We would meet at the same spot on the road every day. It was like we were supposed to meet, but I didn't know who she was. I didn't know where she lived. I didn't know anything about her. All I knew, was that she looked just like you. She was beautiful. She had big brown eyes, and she had a big smile. I told Sammy what kind of car she drove, but that was all I knew about her."

He said, "I know her. She lives right over there." Before I could say a word, Sammy was headed for the front door of the store. He turned back to me and said, "If you want to meet her, come on!"

We jumped in his car, and before I had time to think about what I was going to say, we were pulling into her driveway. She lived less than a quarter mile from the front door of the store. He knocks on her door, jumps back in his car and takes off, leaving me standing there. It was at that moment I realized that he hadn't told me her name. I was so nervous that I almost peed my pants. I thought, this is about to get awkward. If her mom comes to the door, I don't know what I'm going to say. Can your daughter come out to play? Yeah, that would be silly. If her dad had come to the door, I probably would have peed a little. If she comes to the door, will she recognize me as the boy who waves at her every day as we meet on the road? What will I say if she has a boyfriend, and he comes to the door with her? The only thing I knew for sure, it didn't matter who came to the door, I still didn't know her name.

She opened the door and I smiled. I must have said something. I don't know. I really don't remember. I do remember the scent of the perfume she was wearing, it reminded me of honeysuckle. I remember that there was a gentle breeze that afternoon. I remember what she was wearing. Her hair was pulled back in ponytail, and I remember that she was wearing silver-cross ear-rings. I remember the way she stood there as she talked. She smiled at me, and it took my breath away. I melted like a scoop of ice-cream into the asphalt on a hot summer's day. We walked back to my car. I did not know it at the time, but I believe with all my heart, our meeting that Sunday afternoon was by divine design. I had just met a girl who stirred an emotion in my soul that had never been touched before. There was no guarantee that I would ever see her again, but somehow, deep within me, I knew that this was no chance encounter. I'm not sure what role Sammy played, but she was there and I was there for a reason. We were both there at an appointed place and an appointed time. Two birds, thrust upon the stage, dancing in flight overhead to a melody assigned by the Spirit of the Wind.

Ten months later, these pictures were taken and we were married. We moved into a little one-bedroom apartment. Neither one of us had ever been out on our own before, but we knew that what we had was special. Two months later we bought a small two-bedroom house for sixty-five hundred dollars. We made the first payment and moved in without having to make a down payment. The owner financed the house himself. It needed work, so with the help of Pa, that's what your mom and Uncle Jason and Uncle Adam called my dad, we began renovating our little house. We never finished; two months later, I got a new job. We packed everything we owned in a tiny little U-Haul trailer and moved to Hot Springs Village, Arkansas. It was three years later that Nana Debbie got pregnant, and your uncle Jason was born. Here's some pictures of Nana Debbie and Jason when he was just a baby. Before Jason was two years old, Nana Debbie had another baby. This time is was a beautiful little brown eyed girl. Do you know who that was?

"Mommy"

"That's right. Nana Debbie wanted to name your mom Jennifer, so we did. She looked just like you when you were a baby. She had big brown eyes, lots of brown hair, and a beautiful smile. Do you know what a drama queen is?"

'No."

"Well, when your momma was a little girl, she

was a drama queen. She was just like you. But before she became a drama queen, she almost died. When she was six months old, Nana Debbie was working at the daycare provided by our church for working mothers. Because of an infection, one morning your mom developed a very high temperature. In a matter of minutes, your mom's temperature went form 99 degrees to over 104 degrees. Nana Debbie called the office where I worked. I told her as soon as she hung up the phone to call for an ambulance. I left work immediately. I wasn't far from the church. I arrived before the ambulance. When I walked in, Nana Debbie handed your mom to me, she was burning up with fever. Almost as soon as Nana Debbie handed her to me, your mom began convulsing. As quickly as the convulsions started, they stopped. Then your mom's little body went limp. Her eyes rolled back in her head, and she stopped breathing. I held her lifeless body up over my head and cried out, God don't take my little girl. Before I could lower her little body back down, the paramedics rushed into the room and took control of the situation. In less than a minute, they had your mom in the back of the ambulance in route to the nearest hospital, with me and Nana Debbie following right behind and trying to keep up. For what seemed like an eternity, Nana Debbie and I held each other, crying and praying, and hoping that our little girl was going to be okay. Finally, a nurse walked in to the waiting room and said everything is under control. Your mom had a febrile seizure, it was the result of a severe infection. She would spend the next three days in the hospital before we were able to bring her back home. From that time on, everything became a dramatic production if your mom was involved. Here's some pictures of Nana Debbie and your mom when she was a little girl. Here's a picture of your mom and Jason."

Three years later, Uncle Adam was born. Do you know how, when you walk into another room and you don't know that Jax is in there, if he says something before you see him, it will surprise you? Well, Uncle Adam was a surprise for me and Nana Debbie.

Your Nana Debbie loved your mom, she loved Uncle Jason, and she loved Uncle Adam. I think Uncle Adam was her favorite because he was a surprise. Your mom and Jason knew that Adam was the favorite, but everyone knew that Nana Debbie loved me the most. If you want to be like your Nana Debbie when you grow up, then you will have to love people. You can't just love the good people. You can't just love the pretty people. You have to love everybody, and you have to love them unconditionally. That means the love that you have for other people is not based upon their performance. It is not based upon what they can do for you in return. Unconditional love is not selfish. That's one of the reasons everybody loved Nana Debbie. She wasn't selfish, she gave her life away. Most people have no idea what true unconditional love looks like, but your Nana Debbie did. People today are more concerned with their own self-interest than the interest of others. They're selfish.

I don't want you to be selfish. I hope you grow up to be just like your Nana Debbie. She was the kind of woman that every man dreams of being with. That's the kind of woman you want to be. Then one day, a handsome young man will ask you to marry him, and I am praying for that young man even now. I am praying that he will love you as much as I loved Nana Debbie. I am praying that he will see you just like I saw her, as a gift from God. A priceless gift, to be respected, and loved and cherished all the days of your life. I pray that you will love him as much as Nana Debbie loved me. Let's look at a few more pictures, then I will tell you a story and it will be time for bed. We sat in the floor and looked at pictures for what seemed like hours. Finally, I told Jaslynn that we needed to put the pictures away, and I would tell her a story. Since we had just looked at wedding pictures, I decided to tell her the story about when Jesus went to a wedding. As she climbed up into my lap, I asked, "Have you ever heard the story in the Bible about the time Jesus went to a wedding?"

With a look of surprise, she said, "I didn't know that Jesus got married."

I smiled, and said, "He didn't. But, once upon a time, in a land far, far away, a long, long time ago, Jesus and his friends, and his mother went to a wedding. It was a wedding just like mine and Nana Debbie's. One of the most important things about this wedding is that Jesus was invited, just like He was invited to mine and Nana Debbie's wedding, and just like I hope He is invited to your wedding someday."

"Jesus was at your wedding?"

"He was invited. It's kind of like we have talked about when you invite Jesus to live in your heart. If you ask Him to be there, He will. We asked Jesus to be at our wedding, and He was there. Another important thing about this story, is that it was at this wedding, Jesus performed His first miracle. I think that is important because when God brings two people together, and their marriage has God's blessing, it is a miracle. Too many marriages today don't work out because Jesus was not invited and the marriage does not have God's blessing. Since Jesus did His first miracle at this wedding, I believe that tells us something about how important marriage is to Jesus. During the marriage party, the servers ran out of wine. Jesus took six huge jars of water and changed the water into wine. When the master of the banquet tasted the wine, he said, 'This is the best wine I've ever tasted.' He was surprised that the bridegroom had saved the best wine for last. In this story, Jesus was the invited guest, but He was also the bridegroom who showed us that the love He had for His bride, that's me and you, is something to be celebrated. To be loved by Jesus in this life, is a good thing. It's a really good thing, but as good as that is, it is just a foretaste of something better. He tells us in this story that He is saving the best for last. Heaven will be better than anything here on earth. He always saves the best for last."

Go brush your teeth and put your pajamas on, then come back in here and climb up in my lap and let me hold you for just a minute before you go to bed. She hops down and heads to the bathroom. From where I sit, I hear the water running, the toilet flush, and then she comes running around the corner with her pajamas on backwards. She hops up in my lap, and lays her head on my chest. I hold her and smile. This precious child in my arms reminds me so much of her Nana Debbie. I don't want to let go. I don't want to lay her down. I never want to let go. Holding her reminds me of what it means to hold something close that you love so much. After I finally put her down, I sit at the kitchen table, looking at our wedding album, listening to old songs, with tears rolling down my face. I close my eyes, and drift back to the day when we first met. It still takes my breath away. If I could sing, I'd write a song. There needs to be a love song that tells our story. The words begin to dance across the page like angels, choreographed by Gabriel, for the pleasure of God.

When I saw her standing there,

I didn't even know her name.

She looked at me with those big brown eyes.

She smiled at me,

It took my breath away.

Ten months later, her daddy gave his little girl away.

She looked at me with those big brown eyes,

As tears rolled down my face,

She smiled at me,

And said, I do.

It took my breath away.

Some men spend a lifetime, chasing dreams they'll never catch.

But when I get to heaven,

I know just what she'll say.

She'll look at me with those big brown eyes,

She'll smile and say I love you babe.

She brings me to my knees.

She amazes me.

She takes my breath away.

I held her hand one last time.

I looked into her big brown eyes.

She smiled and said, I'm going to be okay.

It brought me to my knees.

God took her from my side that day,

It took my breath away.

Now I hold this little girl.

She has her Nana Debbie's big brown eyes.

She smiles at me, and says, I love you Dandy.

It takes my breath away.

Lord, I miss her.

I miss her smile.

I miss her touch.

I close my eyes and she's still here.

She takes my breath away.

She's always on my mind.

I wonder if she's smiling now.

If she could see me now,

I wonder what she'd say.

Does she still love me?

Does she love this little girl?

Is everything okay?

The music has faded, and the dance is done. I look at my phone. It's 2:14 AM. I'm tired but I don't really want to go to bed. There have been nights that I have fallen asleep and dreamed of Debbie. Those nights have been few and far between. If I could only spend time with her, every night in my dreams, how eager I would be to jump in bed and lay my head down. The truth, however, is most nights I look at her picture, I tell her how much I miss her, and that I still love her. Then I turn and face a queen size bed, without a queen. It's just an empty hole with no bottom, a cold and lonely place. I long for the days when she would lay her head on my shoulder, and I would lay there holding her until she fell asleep. I miss the nights that she wanted to talk, and she would talk and talk until I could not hold my eyes open any longer. I would fall asleep listening to her stories, sometimes long before she reached the end. She was always there when I woke up. It seems like yesterday, and a day, and a lifetime ago.

2

THE SCENT OF A PRAYER

Looking back, I can see it all. We danced in fields of honeysuckle. As the music played, she smiled and stole my breath away. I held her hand the day the music died, and in that moment, we danced like we were eighteen again.

With a cup of coffee in my hands, and breakfast on the table, I cautiously approach 'Sleeping Beauty' enticing her with a feast, fit for a queen.

"Jaslynn. Jaslynn, wake up. It's time to wake up beautiful. I made pancakes. We've got scrambled eggs, and sausage, and strawberries and blueberries for the pancakes. Do you want chocolate milk or do you want orange juice?"

"Chocolate milk, please."

"Okay. Come over here to the table and sit down."

"These are the best pancakes ever, Dandy."

"I made them just for you, beautiful."

"Nana Debbie came to see me last night."

"I'm sorry Jaslynn, what did you say?"

I said, "Nana Debbie came to see me last night."

"While you were asleep?"

"Yes. She is prettier in person than she is in her pictures."

My granddaughter had my undivided attention at this point. I wanted to hear about this dream. I wanted to hear every word, every detail.

"Nana Debbie woke me up. She said we had to be quite so you could sleep. We went into the living room and I got dressed. We talked for a little bit and looked at some of the pictures that you had left out. She told me some things that you didn't tell me. Then she took my hand and said, come on, let's go. There is something I want to show you. We turned the lights off and walked out the front door right into this amazing place. It was beautiful. The sky was so blue, I couldn't believe it. It was like that park we went to that one time, when we floated down the river, and played in the waterfall. We walked through a garden and Nana Debbie picked a tomato. She handed it to me, and told me to take a bite. I bit into it and it squirted Nana Debbie. She laughed. The juice was running down my arm, but it was so good that I ate the whole thing. After that we got a drink of water right out of the creek. Nana Debbie said it was good water.

As we were walking, Nana Debbie talked a lot. She said, "Don't' believe everything your friends tell you. Sometimes your friends will lie to you. The world will tell you that you must fit in. And to fit in you must act a certain way. You must dress a certain way. You must have the right friends. You must do what the boys want you to do. Don't believe it. That's a lie. You are beautiful just the way you are. You are accepted just the way you are. Jesus loves you just the way you are. Don't worry about what anyone else thinks about you. There are more important things in life than how many friends you have, and the clothes that you wear, and what kind of car your momma drives, or where you live." She said that she doesn't worry about any of that stuff anymore.

I just smiled and listened. We kept walking. She kept talking, and I picked flowers while we walked.

She said, "The world will tell you nothing is forever. That's a lie, too. Everything last forever, the good, the bad, the beautiful and the ugly. Everything you do in life remains. There are eternal consequences to everything." She said that Hell is an ugly place. It is full of everything that is ugly, and heinous, things you don't even want to think about, things you never want to see. You don't want to go there. She said that she saw it once, and that she never wanted to see it again.

"What does heinous mean, Dandy?"

I thought for a minute before I answered. "Have you ever been alone in the dark, and so scared that you could not move, and you could not even breathe? It's kind of like that," I said.

Jaslynn smiled, and said, "That's what Nana Debbie said." Then we walked a little more and talked about other stuff. Then Nana Debbie said, "Let's pray."

I asked her, "Where are we going to go to pray?"

She asked me, "When I pray, if I have to go someplace special, or if can I pray anywhere, and who do I pray to when I pray?"

I told her that I pray to God, and to Jesus.

She said, "We do the same here, and we don't have to go anyplace special to do it."

"Is God and Jesus here? Are we going to see them", I asked?

She asked me, "When you pray to God and Jesus, do you always see them?"

"No."

"It's kind of like that here. Jesus is here. He is always here. Jesus is God the Son. He is God, and He walks with us. He is Immanuel. He was Immanuel when He was on earth, and He is Immanuel here in heaven. God the Father is spirit. Nobody has ever seen God, but He is reflected in everything you see. God the Father is everywhere, but He is not limited to time and space. All of creation is a reflection of God the Father, what you see here, and what you see back home. He is in everything that is created, but at the same time He is outside of everything that is created. God the Holy Spirit is here also. He lives in the hearts of everyone here. On earth you see the Holy Spirit of God reflected in the faces of the children of God. It's the same in heaven, the Spirit of God is reflected in everyone here. We are all children of God here. When I pray, I like to walk and I talk to God the Father. Sometimes as I'm praying, I see Jesus walking along side me. We talk with each other, and we talk with the Father, and that's pretty awesome."

"What are we going to pray about?"

Every day I say, "Thank you Father, just for loving me. Because I remember the things I did on earth, that weren't pleasing to God the Father, things I wished that I had never done. I am reminded when I see the scars in Jesus' hands, of the price He paid to show me grace. Thank you, Father, for Your amazing grace. Thank you for the times mercy came running to me. Thank you for the times You carried me when I could not walk. Thank you for the times You lifted me up when I could not stand. Thank you for the times You protected me, and provided for me. Thank you for the times that You held me. Thank you for the cross. Thank you for making a place for me here in Your house. After I say thank you Father, for loving me, I always pray for Dandy, and your mom, and Uncle Adam, and you, and Jax, and Grace.

Let's pray for Dandy, and for your mom, and for Uncle Adam. We will pray for Dandy first. Dandy is sad sometimes. He smiles a lot, but most people don't know on the inside, he is lonely. After I died, and after Jason's accident, life has been difficult for Dandy. He struggles with depression. Most people never see the battle that takes place inside of his heart and in his head. There are times, Dandy wants to go to sleep at night and not wake up the following morning. We will pray for tomorrow to be a good day for Dandy."

"Why don't we pray for all of next year to be good for Dandy?"

"We could, but what if God the Father decides to let Dandy come here tomorrow? If that happens, then tomorrow is all we really need to pray about. If God still has work for Dandy to do the next day, then I will pray for that day to be a good day. So, let's pray that Dandy has a good day tomorrow.

When I pray for Dandy, I always thank God for Dandy. He was always there for me. He walked beside me all the days of my life on earth. I pray that someday, God brings a man into your life to love you like Dandy loved me. He took care of me when I was sick. He showed the world, but more importantly than that, he showed your mom, and Jason, and Adam what the promise; to have and to hold from this day forward, for better or for worse, for richer, for poorer, in sickness and in health, to love and to cherish, looks like in real life. He showed them what true love really is. Most days, I wish Dandy could be here with me, but your mom needs him. Uncle Adam needs him also. Dandy is there is to teach you and Jax and Grace about God, about life and death, and what is really important. Listen to Dandy, because one day his work there will be finished. He'll get to come here, and on that day, I will show Dandy that what God has ordained as good, and put His blessing on, remains forever and ever."

"Nana Debbie, what am I smelling?"

"You are smelling prayers. The prayers of God's children are a sweet aroma. It smells like this all the time here. I'll bet you didn't know your prayers smelled like that, did you?"

"No. That's weird."

"Let's pray for your mom now. Your mom, like

all of us, has made some bad choices in the past. I made some choices when I was a young girl that I wish I would have never made. But sometimes, God will take the bad choices we make, and even though there will be consequences, God's amazing grace provides life's greatest blessings when we mess up. When you get older, the church will tell you, come to God, be cleansed, and leave your life of sin. Then, if you stumble, or when you fall, the modern-day scribes and Pharisees, that's just big words for church-folk, will be quick to point out that you had no salvation experience. You simply experienced the emotions of a guilty conscience. They will say that no true born-again believer could possibly receive grace and continue to sin. God says, 'My grace is sufficient. It's all you need.' The blood will always be enough. Nowhere is it written, in the Bible, that the Father's love is based upon your performance. His love for you, and for all His children is unconditional. Nowhere is it written that your performance, before or after you've been justified by His grace, is required to maintain your relationship as a child of the King. There is no limit to the Father's grace. He may say, I love you, and I wish you hadn't done that. He will never, ever say, I loved you, until you did that. You and Jax are the greatest blessings in your mom's life. She chose life for you and Jax. Most days are tough, but she wouldn't have it any other way. Somedays she is really sad. She misses Jason a lot. She lays awake at night after you and Jax have gone to sleep, and she cries. She thinks nobody cares. She's wrong. Let's pray that she will have a good day tomorrow. Let's pray that someone will make her smile. Let's pray that she will get a special blessing tomorrow, something she didn't ask for, and something she didn't see coming. Let's pray for her thyroid. Hers' is not working like it should. We need to pray that it will start to work like it is supposed to.

Let's pray for Uncle Adam now. Let's pray that he will be a good, good father to Grace, like Dandy was to Uncle Adam when he was small. Let's pray that Uncle Adam will take Grace to church. Before I take you back to Dandy's, is there anything you would like to do?"

"Can we go swimming?"

"Yes, we can, but after we swim, I have to take you back to Dandy's."

Swimming was awesome, Dandy. I could hold my breath and swim under water forever, just like a mermaid. We swam with dolphins and sharks. The sharks we saw were nice sharks, they didn't want to eat us. I touched a whale. It was so big you wouldn't believe it. It was bigger than anything I've ever seen. Under the water were all kinds of different fish. They were all different colors. Some were big, some were really small. It was amazing. Nana Debbie is a good swimmer. She said that she used to be afraid of the water, but she isn't afraid any more. Then she brought me back here. She said she couldn't stay. She had to go back. That was the end.

Wow! Wait! No! I didn't want it to end. Listening to Jaslynn, even though I knew it was a dream, and I wasn't even there, it seemed so real. Why couldn't I have a dream like that?

"Wait. That's not the end. There is something else that I am supposed to tell you. Nana Debbie smiled as she was leaving. She said to tell you that, everything's okay. She loves me. She said, that she still loves you Dandy. She said she misses us, and she really misses you Dandy, but everything's okay. Then she said to tell you that you would really like it there, because that place will take your breath away."

How could it be? She had weaved together the words I had written the night before with a melody, and given birth to a song. Never before had I felt the music move my soul, or life flow through my veins and explode in dance. Like her Nana Debbie, she just took my breath away.

Lord, I miss her.

I miss her smile.

I miss her touch.

I close my eyes and she's still here.

She takes my breath away.

She's always on my mind.

I wonder if she's smiling now.

If she could see me now,

I wonder what she'd say.

Does she still love me?

Does she love this little girl?

Is everything okay?

"Say that again, Jaslynn. What you just said, that part about there was something else that you were supposed to tell me."

"As she was leaving, Nana Debbie smiled. She said to tell you that, everything's okay. She loves me. She said, that she still loves you Dandy. She said she misses us, and she really misses you Dandy, but everything's okay. Then, she said that you would really like it there, because that place will take your breath away."

As soon as Jaslynn finished her breakfast, I called her mom. I said, "Jennifer, we need to talk."

With a hint of sarcasm, a gift I had imparted from the time she was small, Jennifer says, "Okay. What do you want to talk about?"

"I'm serious. Jaslynn had a dream last night. This has got me a little messed up. I've had dreams before, but not like this. She said Nana Debbie came to see her last night. They went somewhere, they went swimming, and then they came back. That's not what has me messed up. Jaslynn knew things that we have never told her."

Sarcasm capitulated to solemnity. I detected a trace of concern in Jennifer's response. "Wait. What do you mean she knew things that we never told her?"

I told Jennifer to meet us at the park in fifteen minutes. I told Jaslynn to get her stuff together. We are going to meet your mom at the park in few minutes. We didn't talk much as I drove to the park. Jaslynn gazed out the window. It was a beautiful morning. I tried to process and make sense of her dream. I not only wanted to believe, I wanted to experience whatever it was that Jaslynn had. As I parked the car, Jaslynn saw a friend playing on the swings. Jennifer was sitting on a bench, waiting.

"Dandy, that's Cassie from my school. Can I go play with her?"

"Yes. You go and play with Cassie. Your mom and I are going to sit over there on the bench and talk while you play."

I walked over to bench and sat down. I took a deep breath, and wondered, if I told my daughter that I believed Jaslynn really had an encounter with her mom last night, would she think I was crazy? I obviously didn't want to confuse Jaslynn, but how can we tell her that maybe she really saw her Nana Debbie, if it was nothing more than just a vivid dream? At this point, I'm worried about Jaslynn, but I'm the one having a difficult time trying to decide if it was more than just a dream. I asked Jennifer, "Do you believe it's possible that the dream Jaslynn had last night, wasn't a dream, but maybe she really saw Nana Debbie?"

"I don't know. Why?"

"Have you ever talked with Jaslynn about your thyroid issues?"

"No."

"She said that Nana Debbie prayed for you last night, and she specifically prayed for your thyroid because it wasn't working like it is supposed to."

The tone of this conversation suddenly escalated to a whole other level of seriousness. The look on Jennifer's face, was as if I had just opened the closet door where she kept her dirty laundry concealed, and exposed every little secret that she thought was hidden.

"What?"

"Oh, there's more," I said. I handed the song to Jennifer that I had written the night before. "Read this."

Tears began to roll down her face. She said, "That's beautiful Daddy. I love it!"

I told her that I had written those words last night after Jaslynn went to sleep. How I had put it in my bible before I went to bed. Then as Jaslynn was telling me about her dream, how she said that as Nana Debbie was leaving, she smiled and said to tell me that everything's okay. She said that Nana Debbie loves her, and that Nana Debbie said that she still loves me very much. She also said Nana Debbie misses us, and she really misses me, but everything's okay. It was what Jaslynn said next that brought me to my knees. She said that Nana Debbie told her that I would really like it there, because that place will take your breath away.

We sat there and talked for what seemed like hours. As I told her everything that Jaslynn had told me. We laughed. We cried, and we both wanted to believe.

3

LIFE ON THE RUN

It was an unseasonably warm spring day. Saturdays are long run days, typically between fifteen and twenty miles, unless it is racing season. Local races in March are common, but there was no race scheduled for this Saturday. I had planned to get up early, and get in an easy ten mile run before meeting some friends at nine o'clock for a leisurely group run. Most days I run alone. Ever since Debbie died, running has been my solace of solitude. I set the pace, and I determine the distance. Running is the only aspect of my life, where I feel as if I have any control. None of us are guaranteed tomorrow.

The healthy have no guarantee of another sunrise, neither do the wealthy or the wise; nor do those in the prime of their life. Every day is a gift, and running is my hallelujah chorus that I sing to express my gratitude for the gift that I've been given. Like the slothful servant, some of us bury our gift and never use it. The music dies, and the dance is over, long before we take our final breath.

Running is my gift. I am not speaking of spiritual gifts; I'm talking about passion. God has equipped each one of us with, and given each of us a passion for something that we can use for His glory. I never gave that much thought when I began running. I was given a gift when I was twenty-one years old, but it was not time for me to use the gift. For thirty-six years I was unaware of what I had been given. Sometimes we find our gift, or we discover it and we don't even realize what we have. Sometimes our gift finds us, and it finds us in the hard times or the dark places of our lives.

In January of 2007 I buried my wife, she was forty-nine years old. For thirty-one years we shared life; love and laughter, tears and heartache, victories and failures. We were the paragon of love, indivisible, a single soul forged from fire and ice. Like a sword in the hand of a valiant warrior, our children conceived in love, became our treasured heritage. Jason, the first-born son was twenty-seven, Jennifer twenty-five, and Adam twenty-one. I speak as a dried-up cistern, overflowing with humility and gratitude; we were blessed beyond measure.

About a year before she died, I began to have some pain in my knee when I ran. I had been running ever since we got married. I never really had any issues with knees, or hips, or feet, or any of the other problems that runners can experience. But this was causing problems.

At this point, I still had not realized that running was my gift. It was a passion, so I began to pray for God to heal my knee. Debbie had been diagnosed with stage four colon cancer. We were trusting God to heal her. Surely, He could heal my knee.

Since losing everything, and moving back to Northeast Arkansas, we were beginning to feel somewhat optimistic about the future. We were paying our bills, and no longer struggling to buy groceries. We had just purchased a new house, and Debbie was making it our home.

Two weeks after we celebrated her forty-fourth birthday, Debbie met with her doctor for her annual exam. Blood pressure, 118/72; resting heart-rate, 57 BPM; she had the body and the physical conditioning of a collegiate athlete. Even though Debbie displayed no obvious warning signs, there was something about her blood-work, along with comments that she made concerning difficulty with bowel movements, that prompted her gynecologist to schedule a colonoscopy. Three days later, I dropped her at the out-patient surgical center for, what we expected to be, an unspectacular procedure. Two hours later, I received a call from the nurse letting me know that everything went well, and that Debbie would be in recovery until the sedation wore off. I arrived to pick up my wife, and immediately I'm escorted to a consultation room, where I am met by Dr. Speight. He didn't waste words. He looked me square in the eyes, and introduced himself as the doctor who performed Debbie's procedure. Like a freight-train that I never saw coming, the next two words out of his mouth broadsided me, and sent me reeling. Nothing could have prepared me for what he was about to say. With a hollow look in his eyes, and an emptiness within his soul, he said, "Its cancer."

She had no family history of cancer. She was in the prime of life. We lived a healthy, and active life-style, complimented with a low-fat, high protein diet. She could walk into a room and turn heads with her smile. His tone was calculated and curt; even so, my immediate response was, "Is it serious?"

Again, he wasted no words, and replied in the same deliberate tone, "I said its cancer."

How do you tell your wife that she is dying? No way in hell, was I going to allow Mr. Congeniality to drop that bomb in her lap as she woke up. Later that evening, while we gathered together as a family to pray, the phone rings. Surgery to remove the tumor had been scheduled. Two days later, the alarm goes off at 3:00 AM. We were both awake. I don't think either of us had slept more than a couple of hours the past two nights. We needed to be at the hospital within an hour. The surgery was successful and she was discharged to go home three days later. The oncology team recommended chemo-therapy to begin four weeks post-surgery.

It was Tuesday, September 11th and getting back to the office, to take care of clients, was not very high on my list of priorities. Taking care of my wife was more important. At this point, I didn't know when I would go back to work. Trying to recapture some since of normalcy, I went out for an early morning run. Like a blanket draped over me, the humid morning air was almost suffocating. It didn't matter. Dripping with sweat, engulfed by the stench of summer running shoes, the rhythmic solitude of every step pounding the pavement, was merely a reflection of me pounding the word of God, demanding answers. Obviously, God was under no compulsion to provide me with the answers. Maybe God was dealing with more important things that morning.

As I walked in the back door, Debbie was resting on the couch and she called for me to come quickly. I hurried to her side. Together we watched in silence and disbelief the breaking news, as the events that morning unfolded on national television. The north tower of the World Trade Center in New York

City had been struck by an American Airlines Boeing 767. The impact left a gaping, burning hole near the 80th floor of the 110-story skyscraper, instantly killing hundreds of people and trapping hundreds more in higher floors. As the evacuation of the north tower got underway, television cameras broadcasted live images of what initially appeared to be a freak accident. Then, eighteen minutes after the first plane hit, a second Boeing 767 turned sharply toward the World Trade Center and sliced into the south tower near the 60th floor. The collision caused a massive explosion that showered burning debris over surrounding buildings and the streets below. This nation was under attack and never saw it coming. As we watched in disbelief, I could not help but feel compassion for the victims as these tragic events were taking place. Somehow, at the same time it all seemed so distant. We had our own tragedy, right there in our living room, overwhelming our lives. And like this nation, we never saw it coming.

From the depths of Sheol, in the silence of that moment, I began to pray. I did not pray for the victims, or their families, or the first responders. I prayed for my wife. Our world had been turned upside down. The chaos and despair in our lives, was more real than what we were watching on television.

Everything changes when you are forced to embrace your own mortality. Our lives, indeed, were changed that day. You choose to either, wallow in your misery, or celebrate like there is no tomorrow. She chose to party. The curse, a finite number of days, became her greatest blessing. From that day forward, she began to give herself away as if she held eternity in the palm of her hands. Others began to see, in her, what had been there all along. Because they saw a life cut short, their eyes were open to see that she was captivated by the beauty of every rising sun, and she always had been. She had a desire to wrap herself, in the fabric of a sky so blue, that even the clouds would blush in her presence. She lived every day with a passion, and a thirst to swallow every drop of life as if she were drinking from a firehose. I am convinced that her celebration of the trivial, and the mundane was so infectious, that it made God belly laugh out loud sometimes, rejoicing that He had given life to someone that truly loved the GIFT. Her zeal for life was dwarfed, only, by her insatiable desire to make others smile.

Four weeks post-surgery, she began an eight-month regiment of chemotherapy. I arrived a few minutes early to pick her up after her initial treatment. I stopped, at the door to the chemo room, and watched as she read to an elderly woman sitting next to her. They laughed and told stories like they were old friends. Later that evening, she told me that Mary, the elderly woman she had been sitting next to during her treatment, had lost her husband to a heart attack the previous year. They had been married sixty-two years, but they never had children. Mary was an only child, she had no family, but this day was the best day of her life since losing her husband. For the next four months, every time I arrived to pick Debbie up, she and Mary would be sitting next to each other. Debbie would be reading to her, or they would be laughing and telling stories like the first time. On this day, when I arrived, Mary's chair was empty, and Debbie looked as if she had lost her best friend. As we drove home, Debbie read a note that Mary had given to Dr. Zingh two weeks prior. Mary knew that her time was near, but she asked Dr. Zingh not to give the letter to Debbie until after she had passed. Two days later, when Debbie returned for her next treatment, I walked in with her carrying a large potted cactus plant. As I sat the plant down in the middle of the room, Debbie announced to everyone, "This is Mary."

Mary had made arrangements to be cremated. She instructed the crematorium to give her ashes to an attractive young woman, if one were to come asking for them. The note that Mary had written to Debbie, asked Debbie to take her ashes and mix them with some potting soil. She wanted a cactus to be planted in the soil.

For the next thirty minutes, Debbie paid tribute to her friend by sharing stories that Mary had shared with her. No one there knew that Mary had climbed Mount Everest, performed on Broadway, and had been barred from most of the casinos in Atlantic City for counting cards. Laughter and tears filled the room that afternoon. Mary, the prickly, barrel cactus still sits near the window today.

We were still believing that God could heal her cancer, surely if He wanted to, He could heal my knee. One evening as I was praying for my wife, I asked God to heal my knee. Runners can be difficult to live with when they are plagued with an injury that prevents them from running. I explained to God, as if He didn't already know, my knee injury was just a small matter compared to cancer. I knew He could speak a word and heal my knee. Even the centurion, in the eighth chapter of Matthew, knew the power of the word when God spoke. He said, "Lord, I do not deserve to have You come under my roof. But just say the word and my servant will be healed." Jesus was astonished by the faith of the centurion. He said to the centurion, "Go! It will be done just as you believed it would." And his servant was healed at that very hour.

Before I even finished pleading my case, God answered with a clarity as real as if He were standing right next to me. He said, "I'll heal your knee, if you will stop running, and start walking." I wish I could say that I accepted His word without question like the centurion, and that my knee was healed at the very moment. I wish that I could say that, but I can't. If you happen to know someone that is passionate about running, you can imagine how that conversation played out. Let's just say that I wasn't thrilled about the condition that God had attached to His promise of healing. I began to plead my case, with great fervor and passion, explaining to God that I was a runner, and not a walker.

I do not like admitting this, but I did not want to become a walker. I would occasionally get upset when someone said they had seen me jogging. How would I cope if someone said, "I saw you walking the other day?" I wasn't a jogger. I wasn't a walker. I was a runner. And I could tolerate a little pain when I ran, but the truth was, the pain was getting worse. Throughout the day I would have a sharp shooting painful sensation from my knee all the way up to my lower back, and these painful sensations were getting worse and more frequent. So, with a hint of pride, I continued to explain to God why I really didn't want to be a walker.

I can only imagine how God must have rolled His eyes as I tried to explain the situation in a way that He could understand, hoping that He would see things from my point of view.

Then He spoke again, saying the exact same thing, "I'll heal your knee, if you will stop running, and start walking."

With a bit of reservation, I decided to test God. I knew that His word would not return void. It says so in the book of Isaiah.

"So shall My word be that goes forth from My

mouth;

It shall not return to Me void,

But it shall accomplish what I please,

And it shall prosper in the thing for which I sent it."

The following morning, I surrendered my pride, and yielded to God's constraint of no more running. I would put God to the test, and walk, for a little while. Prior to this day, even though Debbie was weary from the effects of the cancer and chemotherapy, every morning she would walk through the neighborhood as I ran. After I had run my five miles, I would find her, and we would walk back home together. She stayed within one block of the house, so we were never more than one-half mile from the house when I would meet up with her. But this morning was different, we started together, and we walked together and it was good! For several months, we walked together every morning. We would hold hands like we were eighteen. I would tell her to close her eyes as she held my hand. I would say, "Just breathe and believe. Believe that the breeze in your face is the very breath of God. Believe that God is going to heal you. Believe that God is preparing you to do great work for His Kingdom. Believe that you will share your story with many, and many lives will be touched by you. Just breathe and believe, Baby."

Three months later, her oncologist gave us a bleak prognosis. The chemo was no longer containing the progression of the cancer. Both lungs were irreparably diseased. It was early spring, but her breathing had already become strenuous. Our morning walks had become her anchor and her sail.

On the stormy days, the anchor held, like the wise man who had built his house upon the rock. The rain came down, the streams rose, and the winds blew and beat against the house; yet it did not fall, because it had its foundation on the rock. She stood upon the rock, and her walk would not be moved.

On the sunny days, the breath of God was the wind that filled her sails. Our walks would lift her spirit from the shadows, to rise above the stormy seas, where we would walk above the mountains, dancing like children in the clouds.

I asked if she wanted to go to the beach one more time, before the summer heat and suffocating humidity made outdoor activities impossible. She declined to taint the beach with a sympathy trip. Our memories of the beach were colored with a zeal for life, laughter, running barefoot in the sand, laying beneath a canvass of black, adorned with a million dazzling stars. Those were the memories she wanted to leave me with.

Our morning walks had become shorter and the pace a bit slower, but we both felt the favor of God as we shuffled around the block. On July fourth, from our bedroom window, we watched the neighborhood kids shoot fireworks. July fifth, I called five friends and asked them to pray for a miracle. Two weeks later, with the breath of life laid out before her, waiting to be inhaled; she asked if I wanted to go to the beach. This was no sympathy trip; this was a miracle. We swam in the ocean. We walked barefoot in the sand as the morning sun burst forth in life. We tempted the darkness by counting stars and listening as the waves washed away the worries of life. We made memories like it was our first time.

The last picture I ever took of her, we were parasailing in the Gulf of Mexico. It was a beautiful sunny day, not a cloud in the sky. We were suspended between a summer breeze and winter's chill, like autumn leaves floating in the sky. We were tethered together in a tandem chute. She turned and smiled, I captured an image of her, like an angel, flying high above the clouds.

Four weeks later, after we had finished our morning walk, she was in the bathroom. I was in the bedroom getting dressed. She lost her balance and fell. She broke her ankle in two spots. The ex-rays and MRI's that followed revealed it was worse than just a broken ankle. The cancer had spread, and it had spread to her brain.

For the next 5 months we didn't walk. I pushed her every morning, in her wheel chair through the neighborhood. We would hold hands like we were eighteen. I would tell her to close her eyes as she held my hand. I would say, "Just breathe and believe, Baby. Believe that the breeze in your face is the very breath of God. Believe that God is going to heal you. Believe that God is preparing you to do great work for His Kingdom. Believe that you will share your story with many, and that many lives will be touched by you. Just breathe and believe, Baby."

On Christmas Eve, I pushed her through the neighborhood and we looked at Christmas lights. On January 18, 2007 God took her. In the chemotherapy treatment room today, Mary, the prickly cactus plant still sits in honor of a life well lived. But Mary no longer sits alone. Today there are two. Setting next to Mary, just like before, is the most beautiful flowering cactus plant I've ever seen, in honor of another life well lived.

It was cold and windy the day of her funeral. Darkness came early that evening. I wanted to run. I wanted to put on my running shoes and run again. I thought that if I could run, maybe I could just run away. It was dark, and cold, and I was alone. I went to the Community Center where there was a lighted running path. I didn't care if it hurt. No pain could compare to the pain I was feeling at that moment. As I got out of my car, I saw two young girls in the distance. One appeared to be injured. I walked over to see if I could help. They were cross country runners and one of them had twisted her ankle badly. She couldn't walk. I offered to carry her to her car.

She looked up at me and said, "You can't do that."

As I picked her up, I said, "For the last five months, I have pushed my wife in a wheel chair, and I have carried her because she couldn't walk. Earlier today I carried her for the last time, and then I put her in the ground. I think I'm here for a reason, I'm supposed to do this for you."

I carried her to her car. After she and her friend drove off, I looked up into the sky and said, "I'm going to run now." And I did, without pain. God had healed my knee. It had nothing to do with whether I was a walker or a runner. Most of us, when we find ourselves in a place we don't want to be, we ask the question, "Why me". I learned that night that it wasn't about me. It was all about her. And it was about me being where I was supposed to be, walking beside her for the rest of her life.

I thought God was preparing her for Kingdom work, but God was preparing her for the Kingdom. I got to walk her home. That's when I realized that He was preparing me for Kingdom work. I would be the one to tell her story and give God the glory! I didn't have any idea what that would look like, but I knew that it would be one heck of a story.

In January of 2009 I decided to run a marathon. Up to that point, I had never run a race. I didn't own a Garmin. I didn't know anything about cadence, or stride length, or pace, or heart rate. All I knew was that a marathon was 26.2 miles, and I was going to run one. I still didn't have a clue about my gift. And I certainly didn't see God being involved in me running a marathon. I had no idea that God was about to unwrap the gift and put it on display for everyone to see.

Most of my running for the past six years had been in the subdivision where we lived. Before we had moved into our new house, I ran most of my miles in the cemetery. Running in the cemetery was quite uneventful. I didn't have to worry about dogs, or near misses with distracted drivers. As I began to train for the marathon, I transitioned from running around the neighborhood to running up and down Highway 77, where my primary objective was to get in the miles without being run over.

In September of 2009, I ran my first marathon. By the end of the year, I had run two more marathons. In 2010, I ran two more marathons, one half-marathon, and three 5K races. In 2011, I ran two more marathons, two half-marathons, and four 5K races. I competed in a total of nine events in 2012.

In January of 2013, I began to realize that running was a gift. God had given me a passion for running, and blessed me with this gift thirty-six years earlier. He was beginning to open my eyes as to how I would use the gift for His glory and to heal my brokenness. I began to pray, "God if this is my gift, let me do some great and mighty kingdom work with this gift for Your glory." I wanted to somehow save the world by running, and I was confident that must be what God wanted me to do. Why else would He have given me this gift?

No matter how fervent, how passionate, or how persistent I was when I prayed, all God ever said was, "My son, you are right where I want you to be."

I thought, really? How could I possibly be right where He wanted me to be? How could I do anything of value for the kingdom of God running up and down Hwy 77?

Then in August of 2013 I buried my son. He was a few days shy of his thirty-third birthday. It was a Wednesday morning July 31st, 2013. I went to see Jason, my son. He needed to borrow some money. He had a court appearance that afternoon and he was twenty dollars short. We sat on his porch, eating apples, talking about life, the weather, and guy stuff. Then I handed him a twenty-dollar bill. He hugged my neck and said, "Thanks Dad."

I said, "I love you Bud."

He said, "I love you Dad."

As I turned and began walking to my car, he said something that I'll never forget. He said, "Say a little prayer for me today."

I stopped, I turned around, and I looked him square in the eyes. I said, "I always pray for you, Bud. But there is nothing little or trivial about it." After Jason and I talked some more, about prayer, and how God the Father views the time we spend in prayer, I prayed for him. I prayed with him, and I prayed over him. I hugged his neck again.

He said, "I love you Dad."

I said, "I love you Bud."

Neither of us had any idea that would be the last time we would talk, embrace, hug each other's neck and say, "I love you man". Two days later he was involved in an automobile accident that took his life.

In September, a couple of friends from church came to me and said, "We want to help you organize a 5K race to honor your wife and your son. What do you think?"

My reply was, "Let's do something really BIG. Anybody can organize a 5K event. Let's do something epic. I am convinced that God wants me to use this gift He has given me to honor Him and benefit others. Let's put together an ultra-run, from Jonesboro to Memphis. We will do it to raise money for St. Jude Children's Research Hospital." So, we did. May 2014, I along with twenty of my crazy running friends, ran from Jonesboro to St. Jude.

Later, that same year, the Jonesboro Sun did a

front-page article about the Hwy 77 runner. In 2015, on my sixtieth birthday, I celebrated by running sixty miles. I made the front page of the newspaper again, along with a feature story on the local television station. In 2016, Premier magazine did a feature article about the old guy who ran up and down Highway 77.

Last year I ran from the Arkansas River in Ft. Smith, Arkansas to the Mississippi River in Memphis, Tennessee carrying a USA flag to honor our fallen heroes. I shared my faith on the side of the highway, I shook the hand of veterans, their spouses and the children of many veterans that had given their life serving this country. Television stations in NW Arkansas, Little Rock, and NE Arkansas covered it along with newspapers and radio stations across the state.

My daughter tells me all the time, that I have no idea how many lives I've touched by running up and down the highway. She may be right, I don't know. But, when she says that, I her my Savior saying, "My son, you are right where I want you to be."

A good friend said to me one time, "Life is kind of like running track." I don't know about that. I never ran track.

He said, "When you run track, you just show up and run. You don't get to choose the lane you run in. Someone else determines what lane you run. You just run your best race in the lane that you've been assigned."

Every day I get up and give thanks. I lace up my running shoes. I run down Highway 77, waving and smiling at everyone I meet. This is the lane that has been assigned to me.

By 8:34 AM, I've completed 10.3 miles at an eight-minute pace. I have plenty of time to stop at the convenience store, and grab a Gatorade, before heading over to the high school for the group run. I'm kind of anxious to see who all is going to show up. Felicia had reached out to me, a couple of weeks earlier, and suggested that it would be good if some of us that had not seen each other for quite some time, met for a group run. This would be a time to catch-up on life, and spend time with friends, doing something we all enjoyed doing. On race-day, you may be running with friends, but there is a healthy spirit of competition even between friends. Today, there would be no competition, just friends getting together, and living life on the run. I'm surprised by the number of runners that have shown up. The atmosphere is like that of a family reunion. Everyone seems to be excited about being here. I don't know how she did it, but Felicia has got more runners to show up on a Saturday morning, for a group run, than I've seen at some small-town races.

The pace starts out a bit slower than I am accustomed to, but that's okay, I'm running with friends this morning. The sun is shining; the temperature is ideal; not a cloud in the sky, and for the next sixty minutes, I don't have to be alone. About one mile into the run, I'm up near the front of the group with no idea of what is about to happen. Everyone slows just a bit, not so much as to be obvious, but enough to ensure that I am leading the pack. About a quarter mile up ahead, there is a small group of people standing off the side of the road, in the local chamber-of-commerce parking lot.

Carlos says, "Look. I think we have a group of cheerleaders up ahead."

At this point I don't have a clue as to what's about to happen. But, if members of the local chamber-of-commerce, have come out on a Saturday morning to cheer us on as we run through town, I am going to make a point of letting them know how much I appreciate it. I turn around to the group, and say, "Follow me. We are going to crash this party." Without realizing it, what I did next could not have turned out better, if it had been scripted ahead of time, and everyone given a copy of instructions before our run began. I lead our group of runners into the middle of the encouragers, and began giving 'high-fives' to everyone. I'm smiling and acting as if this is a party, and they have all been invited. It was my mission, at that moment, to see to it that everyone in the group of encouragers, realized how much we appreciated them taking their time on a Saturday morning to come out and cheer us on as we ran by. In my wildest dreams, it would have never occurred to me that this surprise had been set up to acknowledge and recognize me for being the person that is always thinking of others.

Someone called my name. I turned around, and noticed a camera pointed directly at me. Standing next to the camera-man is Lauren Tippett, local news and anchor journalist for KDLC channel 24. The rest of the running group had faded to the background. It was me, the camera-man, and Lauren Tippett, surround by representatives of the local chamber-of-commerce, and the president from First Community Bank.

They were here to tell my story. Four months earlier, I was talking with a friend who mentioned that possibly someone was living in a tent, under an overpass on the edge of town. She had reservations about investigating the situation alone. With the forecast of freezing rain and snow later in the week, I decided to see, if in-fact, someone was living in a tent under an overpass. After making three failed attempts to reach the tent in my vehicle, it should have been obvious to me, maybe this individual did not want to be bothered. That thought never crossed my mind. I am not easily discouraged. So, I decided to walk through the mud, the woods, and the briars for half-a-mile. The closer I got; it became obvious that someone was indeed living in the tent.

Considering that maybe I might not be welcome,

I did become a little bit apprehensive. It was like I was walking into someone's living room uninvited. All of the worst-case scenarios began to play out in my head. This individual may have a knife, or worse, they may have a gun. I am un-armed. I mean no harm to anyone, and my intentions are good, but what if this individual has a violent temper? After taking a moment to assess my surroundings, and reconsider whether or not to go any further, I decided to retreat to my vehicle. From the safety of my vehicle, I called a friend who was an officer with the local sheriff's department. He told me to sit tight, for my own safety, and that he would be there in ten minutes. He said that we would approach the tent together, and see if in-fact someone was living there. Officer Ben Smith showed up to where I was parked, with no flashing lights, and no sirens. As we started walking toward the tent together, Smitty made it clear that he should approach the tent alone, and cautioned me to stay back at least one-hundred feet until he was able to determine if it was safe for me to be there. From where I stood, I could see Officer Smith, talking with the individual, checking his identification, and talking on his radio. After several minutes, Smitty motioned for me to approach. Officer Smith introduced me, as his friend, to Mack Margrett the man living in the tent.

Smitty looked at me, and then he looked at Mack with compassion and said, "What I'm about to say,

I have to say. You cannot legally stay here. If I come back down here, and you are still here, I will be forced to deal with the situation. I don't want to have to do that. So, I'm not going to come back down here unless we receive a formal complaint. I came down here as favor to Dan. So far, no one has filed a complaint. Let's keep it that way."

Smitty knew my heart. Before he walked off, he let me know that Mack had no outstanding warrants. As far as he could ascertain, Mack had no weapons; and there was no indication of illicit drug activity. He knew that I was about to offer help to a stranger, but he advised me to proceed with caution.

It was thirty-three degrees. The temperature was forecast to drop into the teens overnight. The high temperatures for the next couple of days would remain well below the freezing mark. Snow, sleet, or a mixture of sleet and freezing rain were forecast for the weekend. Mack could have been my son. He was someone's son, and he was living in a tent under an overpass. It appeared as if he hadn't shaved in a couple of weeks. His hair was long, and unkempt. His clothes were dirty. I'm certain that he had not showered in several days, maybe weeks. My immediate concerns were, is he hungry, and is he able to stay warm. I could tell that Mack had trust issues, and it may take time to gain his confidence. As we talked, Mack showed me how he had strategically located his tent on the highest spot of ground underneath the overpass. He was shielded from the north winds, and somewhat protected from inclement weather. He had placed two tarps on the outside of his tent to help insulate him from the cold. Inside he had four sleeping bags, two on the ground and two that he slept under. We visited for a while. I didn't want to make him feel uncomfortable. I asked if he would like for me to go and get him something hot to eat. He said that he would not refuse, but I certainly didn't have to do that. I told him that I'd be back in twenty minutes.

I have a friend that owns a restaurant in town, I picked up two plate dinners to go. Each dinner contained two pieces of fried chicken, cream potatoes and gravy, green beans, corn, and made from scratch buttermilk biscuits, and a piece of apple pie. On my way to pick up the dinners, I stopped at Walmart and grabbed a Stanley insulated thermos. I had my friend at the restaurant to fill the thermos with coffee. When I returned, I handed everything to Mack, and said, "This is for you."

He said, "Thank you Dan." But it was what he said next that brought me to tears. He said, "Will you pray for our food before we eat?"

With tears running down my face, I said, "Mack, this is all for you."

He said, "I really wish you would share this with me."

So, I sat there underneath an overpass, on an overturned milk crate, eating fried chicken with my new friend Mack. I gave him the thermos, and told him that I'd be back tomorrow morning, and maybe we could go eat breakfast if that was okay with him.

Mack said that he usually stays up late and sleeps in. He said that he very rarely gets up before eight or nine o'clock. It was cold the next morning. I checked the weather as soon as I got up, it was twenty-three degrees with a fifteen mile an hour north wind. I put on my cold weather running gear, and got in a ten-mile run before going back to check on Mack. When I arrived back at Mack's make-shift camp, there was no indication that he was up yet. I approached his tent cautiously, and begin yelling his name before I got too close. Just as I was about to give up, thinking that maybe Mack had taken off before I got there, I saw movement from inside the tent. I heard Mack's muffled voice from inside the tent, "Dan, is that you?"

I said, "Yes Mack, it's me. Come on, let's go eat some breakfast." Within a few minutes, Mack emerges from within the tent. I had gone for an early morning run, showered, shaved, and put on clean clothes. Mack was wearing the same clothes as the day before. He obviously hadn't showered, shaved or combed his hair. How could he? With no concern for what others might think, I took Mack to the place where I normally eat breakfast a couple times a week. Most times I sit alone. This morning however, I was greeted with condescending stares, by a couple of the regulars, as we walked in. I made it a point to introduce Mack as my friend to those who seemed to disapprove. I was grateful for Tabitha, our server, who treated Mack with the same dignity and respect as Mr. Blunt, the president of First Security Bank, who was sitting just two tables over from us. When Tabitha brought our coffee, I told Mack to order whatever he wanted; this was going to be my treat since he bought last time. Tabitha looked at me and smiled. I'm not sure if it was the hot coffee, the bacon and eggs, the pancakes, or if it was the respect that Tabitha showed my friend, but Mack seemed to relax more, the longer we sat there and talked. We talked for a couple of hours.

Mack shared with me that he had been medically discharged from the army as a result of injuries he received while serving in Afghanistan. When he returned to the states, his wife was pregnant and living with another man. Mack said that was the point in his life, when everything began to come undone. He was suffering from PTSD, depression, and anxiety disorder. He couldn't keep a job. The bank repossessed his car. He lost his apartment. One morning he woke up underneath an overpass, and he'd been on the street ever since. After breakfast, I offered to put Mack up in a motel for the next couple of days, at least until after the extreme cold weather moved through. This would get him off of the street, with a warm bed, a shower, and a roof over his head, while I attempted to see what other resources, if any, were available for Mack. Before we left, I asked Tabitha if she would take a picture of me and Mack. Later that afternoon, I posted the picture on my Facebook page, sharing a little bit of Mack's story and asking my friends to help me show a little kindness to Mack, the man without a home. I never referred to Mack as a homeless individual. There is a demeaning stigma associated with the label *homeless man*. Mack was my friend; he just didn't have a home. And I wanted to help him change that. The outpouring of love from the community was immediate and overwhelming. Over the next several weeks, with the help of friends, we made sure that Mack had food to eat, warm clothes, and a roof over his head. In the days, and weeks that followed, I took Mack to church with me. I prayed with Mack, and I prayed over Mack. A friend was able to put Mack in touch with the nearest Veterans Administrative offices, where he was able to begin the process of applying for the benefits that he was entitled to.

It was this simple act of kindness, and compassion for a stranger, the fact that I had reached out to help someone that others had not even noticed, that lead to me being nominated to receive this community award. After the award presentation, Lauren Tippett explained that the story would air later in the week. With my permission, she wanted to meet with Jennifer, my daughter. She hoped that Jennifer would be able to share insight to my story from her perspective. I knew that Jennifer would tell her mom's story, and that was the story I wanted told. I told Lauren that I thought it would be a great idea.

4

THE DRESS

Sunday after church, Lauren and Jennifer met for lunch. They spent the afternoon talking. Actually, Lauren listened intently, captivated by every word that Jennifer shared as she talked about her mom, and her dad.

From the time she began to talk about her daddy, it was obvious that she was a daddy's girl. She had two small children of her own, but she was still very much her daddy's little girl. The smile on her face and the glow in her big brown eyes as she talked about her dad and her mom, said more than her words could ever say. She was soft spoken, but the volume and clarity of her words would not be denied, as she talked of the fairy-tale love shared by her parents. She remembered living on the lake, feeding the ducks, and her and Jason swimming in the shallow cove behind our house. I sold real estate in a private-gated community. We weren't wealthy, but we lived a very comfortable life style. It wasn't until God spoke to me one day, and told me to walk away from the life we knew, that I realized just how comfortable we had become. It certainly didn't make any since, but I believed that God must have a reason. I turned in my resignation with no idea of what the future would hold. I just figured that God must have a greater blessing in store. To say that I was confused would be a major understatement. It would have been just fine, if God had not blessed us. But I definitely did not expect my act of obedience to lead us into a season of struggle and loss. Over the next eighteen months, the only thing I sold was our rental property, my Benz, and our house on the lake. We traded Debbie's vehicle in on a used mini-van. We were forced to move back to Northeast Arkansas. We had lost it all. When I say, lost it all, I mean everything, including my shotguns and our wedding rings. I wanted to know why. I didn't find out until fifteen years later.

Debbie went to work in a factory. I went to work for a major life insurance company. We struggled financially, but within two years, Debbie was able to quit her job at the factory. She helped me, to build the business, as the office manager. Jennifer talked about her childhood, how she and her brothers had grown up in a family that most of their friends only dreamed about. Their friends knew that there was something different about the way her parents loved each other, compared to what most of them saw at home. Everyone wanted to hang out at our house she said, and she never understood why until she spent the weekend at a girlfriend's house when she was ten-years old. Before that weekend, she had assumed that everyone had parents that loved each other, like her mom and dad. She was wrong.

When she was twenty-years-old, her mom, in the prime of her life, was diagnosed with stage four colon cancer. Her grandpa had died three years earlier, after losing his battle with leukemia. Jason was out on his own, she was living with a friend: and Adam, her younger brother was still living at home. She knew what love was. She never saw her dad make her mother cry. She never heard her dad yell at her mother. She never saw us fight. I'm sure we did, I don't know, but it never happened in front of her.

They had a love for each other that knew no limits, she said. My dad's love for my mom seemed to grow stronger and deeper as mom grew sicker and weaker. I remember dad telling me, shortly after mom was diagnosed, that he and mom had lost everything when they left Hot Springs. At the time he didn't know why, and that bothered him. He wanted to understand. He didn't care if he lost everything again. He just didn't want to lose mom. Money, and business had never been the number one priority for dad. Mom was his number one priority. She always had been. We knew dad loved us, but we knew dad loved mom more. I think that's why we were never concerned as kids that we would ever have to choose between mom and dad. Dad saw her as a gift from God. My mother was a daddy's girl too. My daddy respected her daddy, and he spent his entire life trying to love her more than her daddy did. He also knew that she was God's little girl, and he treated her like the angel she was.

I knew that my dad loved my mom, and he treated her like a queen. But I remember a time when I was fifteen, my independent and rebellious spirit was beginning to emerge. Dad took his last drink of tea, sat the empty glass back down beside his plate, and continued eating. Without missing a beat, mom put down her fork, and got up from the table to refill dad's tea. Overcome by my ignorance and arrogance, I blurted out, "Why don't you let him get his own tea? He's not helpless!" As soon as those words had exploded from my mouth, I knew that I had just stepped on a landmine, and I was about to be crucified. Mom didn't say a word, she just sat back down and looked at me, as if to say, "Oh child, I wish you hadn't done that." Then she looked at dad as if to say to him, "Be gentle. She didn't' mean it."

As dad rose up out of his chair, I realized how disrespectful my words were. I took a deep breath and let it out slowly as I prepared for the beating that I was about to receive. I knew that dad was not going to physically beat me, but I did not dare look him in the eyes. With a simple look of disappointment, dad could cut deeper than a butcher's knife. I knew that I had broken his heart, and been hurtful toward my mom at the same time. As he walked toward me, I could feel the weight of my words pressing down on me, making it difficult to breathe. Jason and Adam sat there without making a sound, like they were watching their favorite movie. In their minds, this would be the scene when the good guy beats the villain into submission. Dad walked over to mom, bent down, kissed her check, and said, "Thank you, Babe." Then walked up to me, set his full glass of tea in front of me. He picked up my half-empty glass, and said, "You're right. I'm not helpless." He filled my glass with tea and set it down beside his plate. Not another word was spoken that evening at dinner. After everyone was finished, I watched from the other room as mom and dad did the dishes together, like always. Except this time, dad washed and mom dried. I learned two things that day; I realized that my mom was the luckiest woman in the world, and someday I wanted to find a man just like my daddy.

Several years later, midway through mom's battle with cancer, we attended the wedding of my cousin Traycee. This was the only other wedding, besides his own, my dad ever attended. I'm not sure if mom wanted him to be there because she realized that she may not live to see any of her children get married, or if she wanted to experience that teenage love one more time before she died. I watched mom as Traycee read her vows, "If I speak in the tongues of men and angles, but I don't have love, I am nothing more than a sounding gong or a clanging cymbal. If I have the gift of prophecy, and can fathom all mysteries and all knowledge, and if I have all faith so that I can move mountains, but I don't have love, I am nothing." Mom was captivated by Traycee and the words she was speaking. Maybe it was Traycee's dress. Maybe she was reliving the moment when she and dad pledged their love to one another, realizing that like an uninvited guest, death was knocking at her door. Dad was gazing at mom, with a smile on his face and a tear running down his check.

After the ceremony, at the reception, as I was dancing with my dad, I asked him what he was thinking as Traycee read her vows. He said that he wanted to be more like my mom, because she had mountain-moving faith, and she had the kind of love that would not die.

Later, while I was sitting alone with mom, I asked her what she was thinking as Traycee read her vows. She looked at me with a smile on her face, as a tear rolled down her check, and said, "If God chooses not to heal me, and He takes me home, remember how much I love you, and how much I love your dad. And if God brings someone else into your dad's life, I hope that you will be okay with that. I will; because I know, that no one, could ever take my place."

My mom gave me a gift that day that I will forever cherish. She told me that she knew how much my daddy loved her. He loved her so much, that even if she were to die, God could bring someone into my dad's life to comfort him, but no one could ever take her place. That's the kind of love that every woman wants. That's the kind of love my mom and daddy had. That's the kind of love I want someday.

Tears fell like gentle rain on arid ground, watering the fields of grief as Jennifer spoke of her mom.

Two weeks after we attended Traycee's wedding, mom asked if we could have a mother-daughter day. I picked her up at 8:00 that morning, she looked beautiful. I remember thinking what a lucky guy my dad was. She was sick, but she still turned heads when we went for breakfast. Like every little girl, one day, I wanted to look in the mirror and see my mom. After breakfast, she asked me to take her to the park. We sat and watched the children play. She talked about how good God was.

Everything in life she had prayed for, ever since she was a little girl, God had given her and more. With my daddy, all of her dreams had come true. I remember, her telling me when I was a little girl that heaven was the place where dreams come true. She took my hand and began to pray. She prayed that someday, I would meet a man like my daddy. She looked forward to the day that she would hold her grandchildren on her lap, and they would call her Nana Debbie.

Then she talked about heaven as if she had already been there. She said it was a place that would take your breath away. It's the place where dreams come true.

After we left the park, she had me take her to a dress shop. The owner greeted her with a smile as we walked in. It was the same shop where mom and I had purchased dresses to wear to Traycee's wedding. We were escorted to a rather large, and private fitting room. Hanging on the rack was my mother's wedding dress. She'd had it altered for me to wear one day. I tried it on, and for a moment I believed in fairy-tales and happy endings. I imagined how my mom must have felt the day she wore it, and I began to cry. I could hear the music play, my daddy walking me down the aisle, and my mom sitting on the front row, smiling like the day when her daddy gave his little girl away. I am not sure if she saw me in the dress, or if she was looking in the mirror, but Solomon's temple, in all its splendor, was put to shame that day, as her radiance filled the atmosphere. For a moment she was eighteen again, she was dancing barefoot in the grass, and there was no cancer.

She never got to see me wear the dress again. She never got to hold her grandchildren.

The day of mom's funeral, dad and I went for a walk, just the two of us. He told me that he finally understood why he and mom had lost everything seventeen years earlier. From the day mom was diagnosed, until the day she died, her and dad lived every day as if it were their last. What the world had called a curse, was one of their greatest blessings. When you live like you're dying, every day becomes a precious gift. The sunrises are a little more radiant. The blue skies are a little bluer. The darkest hour is when the stars shine their brightest. Money and things never were the most important treasures to dad; it was mom. She was always his pearl of greatest price. He valued her, and esteemed her, and cherished like every woman deserves to be loved.

Shortly after my mom died, dad and I were having lunch in a restaurant that he and mom ate in often. As we were being seated, an acquaintance motioned for us to come over. It was a friend of mom's that I had met once before, a long time ago. She introduced us to the friend that she was having lunch with. I'll never forget what she said to her friend, as she introduced my dad. She said, "This is the guy that I told you about who recently lost his wife. They had the kind of marriage everyone should have. They glowed like they were eighteen."

As I sat there and ate lunch with my dad, I marveled at the words this other woman had just shared to describe my mom and dad. Too often women are envious of other women, and eager to tear down and trash talk someone who has something they want. But she just put my mom on a pedestal in front of everyone sitting close enough to hear. I will remember that day until the day I die. Most people marvel at my dads' faith. He lost something that most men will never have. They had a love like no other. I know other men have lost their wives, but no man ever lost what my dad lost. I cannot imagine that any man has ever felt pain as deeply as my dad has.

He smiles as he runs down the highway, day after day. He struggles with depression when he is home alone though. He cries himself to sleep most nights. He's ten-foot tall, and bullet proof. He is my Superman! And when I see my daddy cry, it breaks my heart. He gets up every morning, puts on his running shoes, and takes off to meet the world with a smile on his face. What most people don't know is that shortly after losing my mom, the insurance company that dad had worked with for over nineteen years pulled his contract for lack of production. Dad was grieving the loss of my mom. He and mom had spent nineteen years building a business with one of the largest life insurance companies in the country. The irony is almost laughable, a life insurance company that was more concerned with numbers than life. In just a few short months, dad would have been fully vested, and his book of business would have been his. By pulling his contract, the company was able to enforce the non-compete clause of the agent's agreement. This meant dad retained none of his clients. He not only lost his client base; he also lost his retirement benefits. He and my mom spent nineteen years building a business and saving for retirement. Then he gets screwed over, after my mom dies, by a greedy corporate bean counter, that doesn't give a shit about real people, or real life. Pardon my French, but it's a crappy way to run a business if you ask me.

If that wasn't enough, life decides to kick my dad in the face while he is down. In the months to follow, the stock market loses over fifty-percent of its value. Dad was still grieving the loss of mom. He had lost his book of business and his client base. His future had been taken away when he lost all his retirement benefits by the company pulling his contract. Then, he lost all of his personal savings in the market decline. I think part of the reason my dad cares so much about others who are down and out, is because he knows what it is to lose everything. Dad's depression was becoming debilitating. Most people had no clue, not even his close friends or family. He is seen running down the highway and smiling every day. No one knows the pain and the struggle that is hidden behind the smile.

When Jason, my brother, had his accident, I was afraid that might push dad over the edge. He still had not recovered financially. Emotionally he was still grieving the loss of my mom. Everyone just thought that dad drove the same old car because he was conservative. Nobody knew it, but my dad was broke, and my dad was very broken. I'll never forget the day he told me he wasn't going to be able to keep the house. This was the house that my brothers and I had grown up in. When mom was sick, dad had to refinance the house to cover part of mom's medical bills. The house was the only physical thing that dad had left of the life that he and my mom had built together, and the bank was about to foreclose.

At this point, Jennifer and Lauren, both are sitting there weeping.

My dad, the man who had it all, had become a man with nothing left to lose. When you tell his story, I suppose some people will see my dad as a failure. I hope not. I suppose some will see him as a survivor. I see a man whose passion for running has become a metaphor for life. Sunshine or rainy days, hot or cold, he gets up every morning and puts on his running shoes. He puts a smile on his face, to hide the pain inside. He heads out the door, putting one foot in front of the other, running his race alone. He is my super- hero! That is my dad's story. That is the story that needs to be told.

Maybe the reason that dad reached out to Mack, is because he saw himself, a man with nothing left to lose. Sometimes those who have the least, are the ones who give the most. They are not giving out of their abundance. They are giving because they know what it means to do without. Helping Mack was not the first time that my dad had helped some-one in need, when he was in need himself. This was just the first time that he was being recognized for what he had done.

Through the loss of my mom and my brother, the loss of his business, his savings, his retirement benefits, and eventually his house, the only con-stant that remained in dad's life was running. With a smile on his face to hide the pain inside, dad still gets up every morning, and runs down the highway bringing hope and encouragement to everyone he meets. Drive down highway 77 early any morning and you will see him running, or you may see him standing off to the side of the road with a friend, praying for them or encouraging them. Some mornings, he spends more time loving on people, and praying for friends, even strangers, than he ac-tually spends running. Then she smiled, through the tears, and said, I don't think he would have it any other way.

Later this year, dad plans to compete in his second 100-mile trail run. Sometimes I think he's crazy. I remember the first race he ran. It was a marathon. Most runners choose a 5k race for their first competition. Not my dad. No! He ran a marathon. I thought he was crazy then. I didn't know that being a little crazy was a way for dad to keep his sanity. He had always run. When I was a little girl, he would encourage me to run down the street with him. When I got tired, we would turn around and run back home. Then he'd take off and be gone for an hour, sometimes longer. Before mom got sick, they used to run together. I thought they always would. I just assumed that one day they would be old, and shuffling around the neighborhood together, holding hands.

Even when mom was sick, I believed that God would heal her. The smile gave way to tears again when Jennifer said, never once did I think that God would take her. But He did. Dad tells me that God took her, it wasn't the cancer that took her, but dad can't tell me why God didn't heal her. After mom died, dad ran his first race, the Lewis and Clark Marathon. He ran two more marathons that year. The Mid-South Marathon in November, and the Memphis, St. Jude Marathon, in December. The St. Jude Marathon gave dad a whole new reason to run. Before mom died, dad ran for fun. It was a lifestyle. Health and fitness were important to both my parents. But after losing mom, running became more than just a lifestyle for dad, it became a passion. It was the only thing that gave dad any since of control in a world, in which he no longer had any control. It was his salvation, but it was his demon also. Dad was in a dark place, and running became his drug of choice. He ran to ease the pain. He ran to escape reality. Like an alcoholic with a bottle, or an addict with a needle, dad ran because the blood, the sweat, and the blisters, on a hot summer day, helped to numb the pain that never went away.

The first time that dad ran for the kids at St. Jude, everything changed. Running became a way for dad to do something for someone else, someone less fortunate. Dad believed that he was honoring God, the giver of the gift, and that he was doing something good for others at the same time. My dad always told me that God is the giver of all good gifts. And the gift that He had given my dad was the passion for running. While he was doing something good for others and honoring God, dad was also able to honor the memory of my mom. He knew she would be pleased to see him run for the benefit of the kids at St. Jude. Every year, he ran the Memphis, St. Jude Marathon. And every year, he raised money for the kids at St. Jude.

Running the marathon and raising money every year wasn't enough for dad. His passion for the kids of St. Jude prompted him to organize a 60-mile run from Jonesboro, Arkansas to the St. Jude Children's Research Hospital in Memphis, Tennessee. I knew that he was crazy when he told me what he intended to do. I had no idea that he would be able to find twenty crazy friends to run with him. This was just another opportunity for dad to do good by doing something for the benefit of others while expecting nothing in return. Seeing my dad recognized for his love of others makes me proud to be called his little girl.

After talking with Jennifer, and some of Dan's friends, Lauren knew she had a story. She just didn't have any idea of the impact that Dan's story would have in Northeast Arkansas. Dan had put a name to the face of a problem that most of us had chosen to ignore. Before Dan's story aired, the person living in a tent was just another homeless person that nobody wanted to know. Dan reached out to this man and lifted him up. Then he introduced the rest of us to a man named Mack, a man without a home. He wasn't homeless. He wasn't worthless. He was just a man that most of us wanted to ignore. Today, Mack works in the maintenance department at local hospital. He has his own car, and his own apartment. Since this story aired, the station aired a six-part documentary dealing with the growing number of people, not just individuals but families also, living on the streets in Northeast Arkansas. Business leaders, along with the local legislators, and private citizens have formed a coalition, and received funding through grant money from a private foundation to build a community for *People*

Without Homes. Our *People Without Homes* project has become a model for other communities around the country who are willing to address and lift up the homeless living among us.

5

DANCING WITH ANGELS

T his wasn't the first time that I was about to
do something that would make Jennifer
think that I was crazy. When I told her that I was
going to run sixty miles on my sixtieth birthday,
she thought I was crazy. When I told her that I had
signed up to do a one-hundred-mile trail run, she
thought I was crazy. Ten days from now, I will take
crazy to a whole other level. I will embark on a
200-mile solo run through the Gros Ventre Mountains in northwest Wyoming. This rugged range
of mountains are located just northeast of Yellowstone National Park. They are part of the Greater

Yellowstone Ecosystem. The 200-mile solo wilderness run is organized by Remote Vacation Runs, LLC. It will be an opportunity to disconnect from the outside world for five days. I will be out in the woods by myself with no cell phone, no television, and no technology of any kind. It will be me, the mountain, and my running shoes. Since Debbie died, my mind has been occupied with more questions than answers. I've been told by friends and family, that after the death of someone you love, you eventually learn to accept and embrace a new normal. There was nothing normal about my new life, unless you believe that living with a void as deep as the Grand Canyon in the middle of your chest is normal. Just as I was learning to breathe on my own again, Jason's accident washed over me like a tidal wave, slamming me against the rocky shore, pulling me under and carrying me out to sea again. How pathetic my life must seem, to those same friends and family, when the only constant to which I cling is my passion for running. Like a bottle to an alcoholic, or a fix to an addict, my escape from the pain of reality is my ability to run. For the next five days I will challenge my physical endurance, my mental strength, and my faith in God. The longing within my soul is to draw close to God, as I seek the face of God in the handiwork of His creation. I hope to immerse myself in the mind of God, as I search for answers, that only He can provide, to the questions that haunt me daily.

My two-hundred-mile solo adventure will begin at Prairie Dog Lodge early on Monday morning. The run doesn't actually begin at the lodge. I will be met at the lodge, and transported by helicopter to a remote location high in the Gros Ventre Mountains. For the next five days, the only contact that I will have with civilization is a confirmation signal sent from each of the remote cabins located along the trail.

From the drop zone to cabin one, I will traverse forty-three miles through some of the lower elevations along the trail. Beginning at the base of Mt. George, the first twelve miles of the trail is a combination of dense forest, some extremely narrow and precarious sections of trail, plus some jagged, rocky sections before reaching Hawke Lake. Thirty-one hundred foot of ascent and approximately twenty-eight hundred foot of descent in this twelve-mile section of the trail will expose the legs to a tenuous strain early on the first day. After reaching Hawke Lake the trail crosses a shallow river just north of the Lake, followed by a gentle climb before descending into a narrow canyon where I will have to cross another shallow river. Confronted with a steep climb out the other side of the canyon, the arduous task is made possible by using a system of ropes for support. Continuing to climb, I will encounter some additional sections of dense forest, followed by some steep rugged switchbacks before reaching Mile High Pass. An additional forty-eight-hundred foot of ascent and thirty-three-hundred foot of descent in this nineteen-mile section of trail will tax the legs even more. The next eleven miles of trail, will offer great views of the river valley below as I follow the ridge line until I reach check point one, the cabin at Johnston Ridge.

Day two will begin with a mostly downhill run for seven miles before reaching Golden Lake. After dropping off of the ridge, I will descend back into another heavily wooded section of the trail. Some of the best views on day two are stretched out along the eighteen-mile section of trail between Golden Lake and Normandy Pass. The views of Lovit, Spirit Lake, and Lake Saint Lewis, have been described by others who have completed this daunting endurance challenge, as incredible, incomparable, and places that will take your breath away. After climbing to the summit of Mount Maggie for the high point of day two, I will be rewarded with an easy descent down to Normandy Pass. The fifteen miles of beautiful forest trail from Normandy Pass to check point two, the cabin at Elk Pass, allow for a more subdued conclusion of the afternoon. The ice-cold waters of the mountain spring at Elk Pass will be a great source of therapy for sore legs at the end of day two.

Day three will begin with a difficult climb from Elk Pass to Spencer Ridge, through beautiful open meadows, knife ridges, jagged rocky outcroppings, and some extremely precarious rocky ledges providing more breath-taking views. Fifteen miles in, and like Icarus, I will be soaring close to the Sun as I approach the Eagles Nest on the Ridge. This is the highest elevation on the trail. The next six miles will demand attention to detail, as I tread cautiously along the ridge line over some of the most technical portions of the trail. Once I reach Adams Bluff, I will be forced to place my trust in weary legs, to endure the descent down to Cooper Valley. It may be downhill from there, but that will be no time to get careless. From Adams Bluff, to Lost Creek in Copper Valley, is approximately twenty-one miles. Thirty-nine hundred feet of descent is misleading. Relentless up and down, roller coaster hills before reaching the valley floor will impose a heavy tax on already weary legs. The final six miles of the day will follow Lost Creek to check point three, the cabin at Cody Landing.

Day four will open with a short climb and descent over the Lower Bluff with incredible views of Mt. Jennings and Silver Lake, followed by another short climb and descent over Coyote Ridge before ending at Five Sisters Lake. Ten-miles of mostly wide-open, unhindered trails, will provide some of the most tranquil trail running at its best. From Five Sisters Lake, the trail descends to Buckeye River, where white water and rapid currents offer a single option to reach the other side. A log crossing over the river, where a slip and a fall could be fatal. Once on the other side, I will be met with a steady climb back up to Horseshoe Falls over a rolling, wooded terrain. From Horseshoe Falls I will encounter three shallow river crossings with slow moving currents, typically no more than waist deep. After crossing the third river, the trail descends into the Cypress River valley, followed by a steep, daunting four mile climb up to the top of Elk Peak. From there, a steady descent leads to Kit Kat Junction. Taking caution to avoid the land-mines on this section of trail will impede the pace and forward progress. It is often overgrown with snare vines, waist high eke-grass, and needle-leaf short bushes, leaving any intruder cut and bloodied. It's like trying to run through a cargo net, six-inches off the ground, hidden by waist high Bermuda grass, with strands of barbed-wire crisscrossing the trail. Surviving the obstacle course offers no celebration, or rest for the weary. At this point, I will only be twenty-four miles into day four. The final thirteen miles of the day meander under some of the tallest western-yellow pines in the Gros Ventre Mountains, before reaching check point four, and the cabin at Jackpot Lake.

Day five, if I make it that far, promises to be a day of ease and reflection, beginning with an easy five-mile climb to Russell Bluff overlooking the Little Red River. The next three miles of trail, dances along the bluff, suspended high above the river below, before dropping back down to the valley, and skirting along the river all the way to Jackson Station. Thirty-two miles from start to finish on day five, allows for ample opportunity to enjoy the day and the gorgeous scenery along the Little Red River before reaching the final check point, the cabin at Mini Falls. On that piece of hallowed ground, the final chapter will be written. I will sheath my sword, like a victorious warrior, and collect my spoils. Hopefully, I will be at peace, having taken captive the elusive answers to my quest of questions.

Each cabin is supplied with adequate provisions for an evening meal and breakfast the following morning. Additionally, each cabin will have a bed, a wood stove and a transmitter that will allow for a message to be sent to Remote Vacation Runs each day acknowledging my safe arrival. Sending a single signal will indicate that I have arrived and all is well. Sending multiple signals will indicate that I have arrived and that I'm in distress and need emergency medical attention. Once a distress signal is received, a rescue and recovery team will be dispatched immediately. If no signal is received by midnight, a search and rescue team will be dispatched to the cabin where a signal was last received, and search and rescue will begin at first light the following morning.

Qualifications to participate include submission of medical records, plus proof of having successfully completed at least one, one-hundred-mile trail run; or three, fifty-mile trail runs. A five-thousand-dollar security deposit is required to off-set potential cost if search and rescue efforts are necessary. After completing the two-hundred-mile run, absent the need for a search and rescue mission being dispatched, two thousand dollars will be refunded.

Since the initial run in 2004, nine runners have lost their lives attempting to complete the remote run through some of the most rugged mountainous terrain in northern Wyoming. Seven bodies of the nine who died along the trail have been recovered. Two bodies were never found. It is assumed that the white water and dangerously rapid current of the Buckeye River demanded a sacrifice to appease the mountain gods. Many others have sustained serious injuries, but for those who have completed the run, it has been a life changing experience.

I arrive at Prairie Dog Lodge at 3:00 AM on Monday morning with nothing but a back-pack and water bottle to sustain me for the next five days. As I am climbing aboard the chopper, that will fly me into the drop zone, a thought goes through my head: maybe Jennifer was right. Maybe I am crazy. For the next hour and ten minutes, I wonder if I will be number ten. Will I survive, or will I die with my running shoes on, doing what I love to do? The next thing I remember is Chuck, the pilot saying, "We're here, Mr. Ring. Be safe. Be careful, and have fun."

Ever since the death of my wife, I have walked the empty road, and danced with lonely from dusk till dawn. I have stood in the shadow of sadness as I traced my finger across her name etched in stone. Even so, I could always grab my phone and call someone. I live in an apartment complex with over seven hundred sixty apartments. On this day I have been exiled to this isolated wilderness. The terror of loneliness, like a vacuum is pressing down and sucking the life from my lungs. I solicit the grave, in life and death, to trace her name again. The only contact I will have with anyone for the next five days; will be the confirmation message I send each day as I arrive at each predetermined check point.

The morning air is crisp and cool. I close my eyes and breathe, inhaling the majesty of the mountains, filling my soul from the inside with the splendor of creation. Today's weather forecast is ideal for running. The temperature for the first hour or two should remain in the low forties with the afternoon highs near sixty. After sunset, the temps are expected to fall overnight into the mid to low thirties. The forecast for the entire week is a carbon copy every day, with one possible exception for Wednesday. A high-pressure system off to the northwest, out in the Atlantic is expected to bring extreme cold and snow to the southern portion of Montana. Most forecasts show the severe weather remaining well to my north; however, one forecast shows a 20% possibility of the storm taking a more southerly track. According to my math, that means there is a 100% chance of perfect weather Monday, Tuesday, Thursday, and Friday, with an 80% chance of perfect weather on Wednesday.

The first three miles I try not to think about the next one hundred ninety-seven miles remaining. It doesn't take long for reality to set in. I am out here all alone. One missed step, a fall, a twisted ankle or something worse, and I could become the tenth runner to die out here in the woods. I tell myself to relax, breathe and take deep breaths. Slowly, I begin to focus on the wonder of this magical environment. Five miles in, and I have settled into a comfortable pace. I am actually beginning to enjoy the run. Ten miles in, I spot the first support box. It contains a couple of dried fruit packets, beef jerky, and a couple of protein bars, plus two bottles of water, enough nourishment to sustain me for the next ten miles.

Just ahead, I see a large moose in the woods, about twenty yards off the trail. Moose are among the most dangerous, regularly encountered animals in the world. They prefer to leave humans alone, but if disturbed or threatened they are known to respond by charging with aggression. They attack more people annually than bears, and they are especially aggressive when defending a calf. I remember reading somewhere once, that just before a moose attacks, it may stomp its feet and grunt. The hairs on its hump are raised, and its ears are laid back, much like a dog or cat. It may even lick its lips. I am no expert on moose, but if I can see the hair on the back of its neck, I'm too close. I decide to sit and watch for a while. Not really sure how long this might take, I find the largest tree between me and the moose, just in case Bullwinkle decides to get aggressive. Within a few minutes, the moose looks in my direction, nods her head, and wanders off slowly in the opposite direction. I sit for just a minute, trying to take it all in, before continuing along the trail.

I make it fifty yards down the trail, before stopping dead in my tracks again. This time, I am overtaken by the most picturesque view of a mountain lake that I've ever seen. It is like nothing I've ever seen before. If there were mountains and lakes in the Garden of Eden, I'm sure this is what it would have looked like. The water on the far side appears to be polished silver, reflecting a mirror image of the shoreline and sky above. The near side of the lake, the water is so blue it almost hurts your eyes to look at it. I am seeing something that very few other men have ever seen, and I'm overwhelmed. I walk to the water's edge, I see my reflection in the crystal-clear blue water, and I'm amazed. Not wanting to leave, I'm forced to make a choice. I strip off all my running clothes, my socks, my shoes, and my shorts. Here I am, all-natural, standing on the edge of a mountain lake. It's cold, and I know the water is freezing, but I may not have the opportunity to go skinny dipping in a mountain lake again, that most people have never even seen.

WOW! That was the most exhilarating sixty seconds of my day. Nothing gets your blood flowing like swimming naked in freezing water. Now I'm ready to put my running gear back on and start moving again. Before I've even completely dried off, I reach the first river crossing. Immediately upon exiting the water, I begin climbing. Just as I reach the top of the ridge, I spot the second box. It contains more of the same as what was in the first box. This marks the half way point of day one. After feasting on more beef jerky, protein bars and dried fruit, I begin my decent down the back side of the ridge to the cannon floor where I cross the river for the second time. As soon as I emerge out of the river, I have a choice. The trail follows the river for about a mile before circling back and beginning a gradual climb up the ridge through a series of switchbacks. Option two is a steep and rocky, near vertical climb up the ridge with the aid of guide ropes on both sides of the trail for support. Option two is definitely intimidating, and to say the least, a little scary; but, given the choice of four miles of switchbacks or one-half mile of steep and rocky, I decide to go steep and rocky. The first two hundred yards of climbing would be nearly impossible without the ropes to hold on to. Reaching the end of the support ropes doesn't mean the climb is over, is simply means the rate of incline isn't quite as steep.

There is still over 7500 feet of elevation change before reaching Mile High Pass. At Mile High Pass I spot the third support box. I'm ready for a break. At this point, I am hoping for something more than beef jerky and dried fruit. Reality declares to the trespasser in the woods, hoping for something and receiving it, are not congruent paths. The path to which I'm destined to follow yielded no choice. It provided more beef jerky and dried fruit.

The next eleven miles of trail followed the ridge line with some exposed sections of trail and great views of the river valley below. I am captivated by the views below me, but what I really want to see is a Holiday Inn. Again, reality declares that the path I'm on will not lead to a Holiday Inn. As the vision of clean sheets, and a hot shower fade away, I see the cabin. My first thought is, that's not a Holiday Inn. It's a cabin up here in the middle of nowhere; and for a solitary man, it is a welcoming site.

From the outside, I'm already impressed. As I open the door, my initial observation is confirmed. It's not a Holiday Inn. Up against the back wall is a twin-size wooden bed frame, with no mattress or box springs, just a thick gymnastic mat over the wood frame. There is a small table with two chairs in the corner; a wood burning stove for heat; a cast iron skillet; and two 5-gallon water canisters; enough for drinking, making Gatorade, and coffee. In one storage container, I find Gatorade mix and coffee packets, along with two apples, four bananas, an onion, carrots, a baguette, half a dozen eggs, oatmeal, cinnamon, and honey. In the second container is a steak and half pound of thick cut bacon, some green beans, and six small potatoes. Solar panels on the roof of the cabin provide enough power to recharge my Garmin and my Knuckle lights, in addition to providing adequate light inside the cabin. There is no running water inside, but there is an outside shower. The first thing I decide to do is to build a fire in the stove. Then I take a quick outside shower, and wash out my running clothes. I hang them on the back of a chair and set it near the stove so they will dry. I throw the steak in the cast iron skillet and set it aside. Next, I put the potatoes, carrots, onion and green beans in a pot, cover them with water, and bring it to a boil on the stove. After the vegetables are cooked, I set the skillet on the stove and sear the steak. With food in my belly, a warm fire, and a place to lay my head, day one has been a good day. As soon as I have finished eating, I transmit the confirmation signal acknowledging that I have arrived safely at the first check point.

If the altitude has not affected my internal clock, I'm laying here in the dark, thinking it must be pretty close to 5:00 AM. Either way, the temperature inside the cabin has dropped, and I need to put another log or two in the stove. After checking my Garmin, I was able to confirm that my internal clock is working properly. It's 4:55 AM. The sun will be up shortly. It's time to get up, fix breakfast, and get an early start on day two. First thing I do is to boil some water for coffee. Then I'll fix some oatmeal. I've got butter, honey, cinnamon and apple; it's almost like being at home. After three cups of coffee and oatmeal, I fry the bacon, the eggs; and I make egg sandwiches with the rest of the baguette. Still hungry, I decide to go ahead and eat one egg sandwich. I pack the other two along with the bananas, in my back pack to carry with me.

As soon as it is light enough to see the trail, I decide to leave the cabin. Before I leave, as I'm finishing my last cup of coffee, I talk with God. Maybe on this day, Lord, I will see You somewhere along the trail, just like Peter, James, and John experienced the transfigured Christ on the mountain top. Maybe Moses and Elijah will there too. We will talk, and I will have all my questions answered. Maybe, the Spirit of God will reveal Himself to me, and tell me things I long to hear. The air is cool and crisp. I am anticipating another day of perfect weather for running. Day two begins with a mostly downhill run for seven miles until I reach Golden Lake. Almost immediately after dropping off of the ridge, I find myself back in a heavily wooded section of trail. Not long after leaving the lake I spot my first supply box of the day. Just like day one, it contains dried fruit, beef jerky, and a couple protein bars, along with bottled water. At this point, I am grateful for the fresh fruit and egg sandwiches

I packed before leaving the cabin. The eighteen-mile section of trail from Golden Lake to Normandy Pass provides some of the best views on day two. Just beyond the first supply box, I begin the steep climb out into the Mount Maggie backcountry. Before reaching the summit, there are three more mountain lakes with incredible, untouched, natural beauty, revealing the sacredness of His holy sanctuary. After climbing to the summit of Mount Maggie for the high point of day two, it's an easy descent down to Normandy Pass. Once I reach Normandy Pass, it's approximately fifteen miles of beautiful forest trail to check point two, the cabin at Elk Pass. The ice-cold waters of the mountain spring at Elk Pass are a great source of therapy for sore legs at the end of day two.

It's been another good day, but at the end of day two I'm feeling a little angry, and disappointed. I had signed up for the wilderness run looking for answers. I've searched for God all day long, and I didn't find Him. I have experienced the awe of His glory, displayed in the beauty of creation; but, I am lonelier than I've ever been. Maybe dying out here on the trail tomorrow wouldn't be such a bad thing after all.

Day three begins much like the previous two days. It appears as if the severe weather stayed to the north providing another great day to run. This day, however, would be the longest day of my adventure. Today's run consists of fifty-three miles through some of the most technical sections of the entire two hundred mile plus course. For two days I had searched for God in the remote mountainous region of Wyoming. For two days, I longed for answers. Isolated and alone, I began to accept the fact that I may not find what I was looking for. My mind was full of questions, but the trail was not yielding any answers. I am fifteen miles into the day when I reach Eagles Nest on the Ridge. I am at the highest point of the trail. This is no place to get careless. The next six miles of trail are the most rugged, and technical section of the entire trail. Every step is guarded at this point, a miss step here would undoubtedly result in undesirable consequences.

As I'm falling, I remember thinking, this is not going to end well. I am going to hit my head. I'm going to die. I'm going to be number ten. Time stopped. There was time to embrace the inevitable, but no capacity to prevent the undesirable. Time to reclaim hurtful words spoken in haste, but no time to reach the ones I'd hurt. Time to say the things I longed to say, but no one here to listen. In this life I did not get the answers I was looking for. In the next life, I will ask the questions, and I will have my answers. There was no bright light. There were no loved ones to welcome me. I was not overwhelmed with a feeling of love. There were no vivid colors, just blinding darkness and unbearable pain. My head felt like it was split wide open. I couldn't move. I thought, if I don't check in tonight, they will send a search and rescue team looking for me tomorrow. I wondered what they would find. It was obvious that my leg was broken. I could feel bone protruding through the flesh. There was blood running down my face, my head was throbbing. I knew this was serious. I drifted in and out of consciousness with no concept of time. I felt as if I were trapped somewhere between life and death. At times, I could see my broken body below, but I felt nothing. There was an overwhelming void of any sensation. Blood covered the ground. Seeing the gash on my forehead and the bone poking through the flesh of my right leg, if somehow, I did survive, I knew that my life would never be the same. I opened my eyes, but I was still unable to move. The pain was excruciating. This time, kneeling beside me was the woman I had seen at the cemetery weeks before. She was weeping, and holding me. She was wiping the blood from my face with her tears. As I looked into her face, I felt no pain. What I felt was an overwhelming since of unconditional love.

I remembered a dream that I had years before. The day I died, Debbie and I ate breakfast in an open-air café on the beach. We sat there watching the sun rise, like a ball of fire erupting from a watery grave. The God of heaven, who raised the Son, with a word of LOVE, was summoning the sun to rise again. The waters came no further than He commanded, and dared not cross the line He had drawn in the sand. We marveled at the majesty of His supremacy. I ran the Maui Marathon, with the wind in my face and the sun at my back, surrounded by the beauty of the Pacific Ocean. Then we made love like we were eighteen. We watched from Lahaina beach, as the sun drifted below the horizon, surrendering to a relentless grave. The stars began to roll back the darkness, and reveal the hidden glory of the heavens above. I reclined at her bosom, suffocated by unspeakable peace, and a scandalous love. With a smile on my face, I took my final breath.

Just before I lost consciousness, I noticed a young girl holding my hand. The angel from the cemetery straightened my leg, the pain and darkness returned. I had seen my broken body, but felt nothing. I had felt unconditional love as she held me in her arms. And now, I am overcome with excruciating, and unbearable pain. It's dark and I'm alone; this must be Hell. The next thing I remember is lying in a bed. I thought maybe that I had been rescued. I had no idea where I was, but there was something strangely familiar about this room and this bed. The young girl was kneeling beside the bed, and she was praying for me. The woman was putting something to my lips. She said that I should eat because I will need strength, and she told me to rest. She took hold of my hand and declared a word as if it had already happened. She said, "Close your eyes. Just breathe and believe. Believe that the breeze in your face is the very breath of God. Believe that God is going to heal you. Believe that God is preparing you to do great work for His kingdom. Believe that you will share your story with many, and many lives will be touched by you. Just breathe and believe." All throughout the night, I drifted in and out of consciousness. Every time I opened my eyes, she was there, caring for me, weeping over me, praying for me. At one point during the night, I woke up, but she was no longer caring for me. She was lying next to me, and I was holding her, like we were eighteen.

When I regained consciousness, she was gone. I was in the cabin, but I was alone. I didn't feel any pain. Confusion was my only companion at that point. I walked outside. I was obviously still somewhere in the mountains, but I was not on the trail. I was scratched and cut up, but I was able to walk. Immediately my mind begins to betray me again. I see a man walking toward me, and he is smiling. It looks like my dad. He says, "You took a pretty good fall, but I'm here to take you home. Follow me." I looked at my leg. There was a scar where the bone had been sticking out. I felt my forehead. I could feel the scar, but there was no gash. I didn't say it out loud, but I thought to myself. If I had a choice, I would rather go home with the angel that I spent the night with last night. I would follow her anywhere. Where ever she wanted to go; I'd follow her. I assumed that I must be dead, because nothing is making sense at this point. Of all the things I could have said, I asked, "If I'm dead why do I have these scars?"

My dad smiled, and lifted his shirt. He showed me his scar. He said, "When I got here, I thought that I would lose this scar."

I began to weep. I knew the pain and the shame behind his scar. We all have things in our past that we wish weren't there. Things we wished we had never done. Things we wished we had never said. Things that we have washed in the blood of Jesus, thinking that someday they would be gone for good. I didn't understand. If the past has been washed away, then why would our scars remain?

He said, "I stood before Christ and asked the same question. He showed me His scars. He said, 'I chose these scars for you.' Every day I see my scar; it's always there to show me what amazing grace truly is. Every day I see His scars. Those scars reveal the depth of His love, and remind me every day of the price He paid to ransom me."

Then my dad asked a question, he asked me what I remembered. I began telling him how I was running along the ridge when I tripped and fell. He interrupted me by saying, "Before that." I began telling him about planning the trip. Again, he interrupted me and said, "Before that." Every time that I digressed down memory lane a little further, he insisted that I back up even more. Finally, he asked, "What is the first thing that you remember?" For hours we walked and talked. We laughed and we cried. I remembered things that I thought I had forgotten. As the sun was setting, the light that had revealed the truth, yielded to the grave, he looked at me and said, "I love you son. Those are your scars."

I said, "Am I dead?"

He said, "No! You're not dead. This is not a dream. This is not a near-death experience, even though you almost died."

I said, "If I'm not dead, and this is not a dream, and it's not a near-death experience, then what is this?"

"It's more like a revelation. You have been given a gift. Before you die, you will have a near-death experience. Everyone does. Some live to tell about it, most don't. The vision you have just before you die is a glimpse of eternity. Visions filled with vivid colors, bright lights, and loved ones before you die are glimpses into Heaven. Feelings of emptiness, loneliness, darkness, torment and anguish are merely glimpses of the pain and isolation of being separated from God for all eternity. Death itself is not something to be feared. Death is simply a transition from the only life you know, to a deeper, more vivid existence.

As a child, you spent the first nine months of life in a world created to protect you, and prepare you to live in the world as you know it now. Your mother and I loved you before we ever held you. We talked to you, we even called you by name. If you were restless, your mother would sing to you, and almost immediately, you would calm down. You grew, you lived and you played in the only world you had ever known. We desperately longed for the day when you would be with us, so that we could show you just how much we loved you. You had no idea what was waiting for you on the other side. How could you? The vivid colors, the sounds, the smells, or the things you would hear and feel. How could you possibly know the beauty of the rising sun, or the sound of ocean waves crashing against the beach? How could you possibly know what it felt like to walk barefoot through the grass on a summer day? You were loved, but you had never been hugged. You had never seen a million stars light up the night sky, from the bed of a pick-up truck, down a country road in rural Arkansas. You had never swum in a creek or played in a mud puddle. You never stood outside on a winter's day and caught snowflakes on your tongue. The world that you lived in had everything you needed, but there was so much more that you didn't even know existed.

And then one day, you died. You died to the only life, and to the only world you had ever known. And death gave way to birth. You could never have transitioned to this world, if you had never died to that world. For those who choose life in this world, death is merely a transition to the better world. But for those who choose to be their own god, in this world, death gives way to a darker world. That darkness is more vivid and intense than you could ever imagine. It's a world where the only light that ever shines, is a distant memory, from a time long ago. It has been said, *It is as if they were stillborn*. The only light, and the only love, and the only laughter for all of eternity, is in the mind of that pitiful soul who knows nothing now except solitude and darkness.

It's a choice. It has always been a choice. For two thousand years the world has tried to complicate religion and salvation. Our Father never intended for it to be complicated. John got it right in his gospel when he said, "In the beginning was the Word, and the Word was with God, and the Word was God. He was with God in the beginning. Through Him all things were made; without Him nothing was made that has been made. In Him was life, and that life was the Light of men. The Light came to bring light to a dark world. That Light penetrates the darkness, and the darkness will never overcome the Light. The true Light that gives light to every man had come into the world. He had come into the world, and though the world was made through Him, the world did not know Him. He came to His own, but His own rejected the Light. But to all who would embrace the Light, to those who would believe on His name, He gave to them the right to become children of Light, children of God – children born not of natural descent, nor of a human decision or a husband's will, but children born of God."

Then he said something I will never forget. I don't think I'll ever forget a single word he said to me that day, but what he said next resonated with a new-found clarity. He said, "When you get back, remember this. The paradox of life is that you have to die, before you ever truly learn to live. You must be born again. It really is that simple."

I slept very little that night. All I could think, as I lay there, was how much I loved Jason, my son. From the time he was born until the day he died, I wanted him to know how much I loved him. After his accident, a friend of his made a point to come and talk with me after the funeral. He said that Jason often talked about how much he loved me, but the one thing that he said Jason talked about even more, was how much he was loved by me. He said, "He not only loved you deeply, Mr. Ring, but he knew how much you loved him." As I laid there, I realized that this, is what I was to my father. He loved me and I knew it. I tried to comprehend that if I had loved my son without limits, and my father had loved me without limits, how much more God the Father loved me. I struggled to wrap my mind around the concept of how deep, how high, how broad the Fathers' love must be. Restrained by the self-imposed restrictions we place on our own comprehension; I'm forced to concede that I could not possibly know. I can't sleep. I'm still not sure what is real and what's not. I know I fell. I know that I hit my head and broke my leg. I consider the possibility that if I do doze off, l could wake up in the morning all alone, unable to walk, and covered in a pool of my own blood. I know one thing; I'm going to tell my dad goodnight. I am going to tell my dad that I love him. I may not get this chance again. I say, "I love you dad."

He says to me, "Goodnight son. I love you too."

I lay there and ponder if maybe this could be heaven? I wake up to the smell of coffee. I don't see my dad, so I get up, pour a cup of coffee and step outside. Dad is sitting there on the porch, drinking his coffee, and talking with someone I don't recognize. The sunlight is so bright, it literally hurts my eyes to look. As I walk toward my dad, the light intensifies but the stranger seems to fade away. Before I can even speak a word, my dad just smiles, and says, "How did you sleep?"

I had slept just fine, but I had other things on my mind. If I wasn't dead, and this wasn't a dream, whatever it was, I had questions. I had deep theological questions. Questions about why Debbie had to die. Where was God when Jason died?

I wanted to know; did God see a cross before He planted a garden. Did He look beyond the garden to the cross when He said, "Let there be light?"

What happened between the end of the sixth day, when God said, "It is very good", and evil comes to the garden? Man is deceived, and what was very good, ends up being very broken.

Was Lucifer evil when God created him, or was he very good in the beginning? Did God see in Lucifer, all the evil the world would ever know before He spoke him into existence? Did evil exist from the beginning? There was a tree of the knowledge of good and evil even before man had sinned. Did evil already exist? Was evil a part of God's creation?

If God saw the cross before He planted the garden, why did He even create Lucifer? I understand that God is omnipotent. He is all powerful. I understand that God is omnipresent. He is everywhere. I understand that God is omniscient. He is all seeing. He sees everything because He is omnipresent, He is everywhere. But, does He see what has not happened yet as if it has already happened? If He does, then why Lucifer? If God saw, before the foundation of the world, the evil intent of man's heart before the flood, and the evil of Sodom and Gomorrah, then why create Satan?

I want to know if Adam and Eve are together in heaven. I want to know if what God has ordained and blessed is eternal. I want to know if what God has joined together, if what was once two, and has become one, by the hand of God, remains one;

or, does death undo what God has joined together. How far does redemption reach?

Dad just smiled again. He held his hand up and said, "Easy Triger."

I said, "What?"

He said, "The first time Jason said that to me, I nearly lost it. We've got lots of ground to cover and two days to do it. Let's eat a little breakfast. Then we will walk and talk. I'll answer all your questions."

As we began to walk, he said, "If you sow sparingly you will also reap sparingly, but whoever sows generously will also reap generously. Each one should give what he has decided in his heart to give, not out of regret or compulsion. For God loves a cheerful giver. And God is able to make all grace abound to you, so that in all things, at all times, having all that you need, you will abound in every good work."

Then he said, "If you owned two cows, and God asked you to give one of your cows to the church, that's not a tithe. That's fifty percent of the all the cows you own. Likewise, if you neighbor has two cows, and God asked your neighbor to give ten percent of all the milk produced by his two cows to the church, that is a tithe. You will have to decide in your own heart whether or not you trust God. You have free will, and you may choose to keep both cows, and like your neighbor tithe ten percent of all the milk your cows produce. Or you may choose to trust God, and do what He has asked of you, even though He has not asked the same from your neighbor. If you decide in your own heart to trust God, and to give half of all the cows you own to the church, God will not love you more. If you keep both cows, God will not love you less. But you will never know why God had asked you to do something that He did not ask your neighbor to do.

Suppose you give one cow to the church. Is God able to bless the cow you kept, so that she produces more milk than she did before? You may never know this side of heaven the lives you saved by giving one cow to the Kingdom of God. What if God blesses you with a bull, and your cow has a calf, and you mate your bull with the neighbor's cows. You receive a calf and your neighbor keeps one calf. If God asked you to do something, does it really matter if He did not ask the same of your neighbor?"

I felt kind of like the disciples when Jesus talked in parables. I think somehow the cows and the farmer may have something to do with Debbie's death, but I'm not sure. I wanted to say, "Yeah, so what's your point in this story dad?" I continued to listen without saying a word, hoping that there would be a life application somewhere to his story.

Dad continued to weave bible stories into our conversation. He said, "You do understand the kingdom of heaven is like a landowner who went out early in the morning to hire workers for his vineyard. He agreed to pay them a denarius for the day and sent them into his vineyard. About nine in the morning he went out and saw others standing in the marketplace doing nothing. He told them, 'You also go and work in my vineyard, and I will pay you whatever is right.' So they went. He went out again about noon and about three in the afternoon and did the same thing. About five in the afternoon he went out and found still others standing around. He asked them, 'Why have you been standing here all day long doing nothing?' He said to them, 'You also go and work in my vineyard.' When evening came, the owner of the vineyard said to his foreman, 'Call the workers and pay them their wages, beginning with the last ones hired and going on to the first.' The workers who were hired about five in the afternoon came and each received a denarius. So when those came who were hired first, they expected to receive more. But each one of them also received a denarius. When they received it, they began to grumble against the landowner. 'These who were hired last worked only one hour,' they said, 'and you have made them equal to us who have borne the burden of the work and the heat of the day.' But he answered one of them, 'I am not being unfair to you, friend. Didn't you agree to work for a denarius? Take your pay and go. If I want to give the one who was hired last the same as I gave you, don't I have the right to do what I want with my own money? Or are you envious because I am generous?'"

He looked at me, and said, "What do you think?"

I said, "I don't think you have answered my question."

He just smiled, and without missing a beat, he asked, "Do you remember the time Peter turned and saw that the disciple whom Jesus loved was following them? This was the one who had leaned back against Jesus at the supper and had said, 'LORD, who is going to betray you?' When Peter saw him, he asked, 'LORD, what about him?' Jesus answered, 'If I want him to remain alive until I return, what is that to you? You must follow me.'"

He said, "Life is kind of like running track son. Each runner is assigned a lane to run in. You show up prepared to run, but you don't get to choose what lane you run in. Your lane is predetermined before you ever show up at the starting line. You should listen to God. He will tell you what to do. He may not ask of you the same thing that He asks of your neighbor. So, pray that you have eyes to see and ears to hear. And when He speaks, trust Him. God may bring someone else into your life Dan, but He may not. If He does, you will know it."

For the next two days we walked and talked. I never asked where we were going. I was drawn in by every word my dad had to say.

He hugged my neck, and said, "I love you son."

I said, "I love you dad."

As he walked away, I stood there unable to move, and unable to speak. He turned around and said, "Remember everything that I've told you. When you started this journey, you wondered if it would change your life. I hope it has. Now, I will tell you what you really want to know. It was her that wiped your wounds with her tears. She cared for you because you had cared for her. She prayed for you and she took care of you. She is waiting for you, but it is not your time just yet." Then he was gone.

I turned around, and walked into the cabin, not knowing what day it was. I didn't know how much of what I remembered from the past few days was real, if any of it was. All I wanted to do, was to lay down and sleep. I had no idea where I was, but I knew that I wasn't home. And I remembered the first thing dad said to me, "I'm here to lead you home." As I head toward the bed to lay down, I realize that I'm falling. I remember thinking, this is not good. I am going to hit my head. I'm going to die. My head felt like it was split wide open. I couldn't move. It was obvious that my leg was broken. I could feel bone protruding through the flesh. There was blood running down my face, my head was throbbing. I knew this was serious. I drifted in and out of consciousness with no concept of time. I felt as if I were trapped somewhere between life and death. Blood covered the ground.

I opened my eyes, but I was unable to move. And then it was over. I heard a voice. It said, "We're losing him." I see my broken body lying on the ground, covered in blood. The EMT's are frantically trying to save my life.

I hear another voice. It says, "It's not your time."

I hear my dad saying, "Here in this place, day and night exist, but there is no record of time."

Then I hear Jennifer screaming my name. Daddy! Daddy!

I wake up in the hospital, Jennifer and Jaslynn are there. I can't speak, but Jaslynn says to me, "You're going to be okay Dandy. Everything is going to be okay." I'm drifting away again. The next thing that I remember is being back home, and wanting to come back to this place.

So, we do. All of us, we come back. Once we reach the clearing where the cabin is, Jax sees Jason and takes off running. Debbie sees Jennifer and Jaslynn, and she starts running toward them. I am watching from a distance, with tears rolling down my face, but I can't move, and I can't speak. Jennifer looks back, and says, "Daddy. Daddy, come on." It's like I'm not even there. I look down. The ground is covered with blood. My leg is broken; it's no wonder that I can't move. I put my hand to my head. I feel the split in my skull, blood runs down my arm, and drips to the ground. I surrender to the pain and the darkness once more.

6

THE FALLEN LIMB

It's 4:00 AM. The phone is ringing. An unknown number, but something compels Jennifer to answer the call. With one eye opened, suspended somewhere between sleep and death, she manages a muffled, "Hello."

The voice on the other end is Captain Dawson with Gros Ventre Mountain Search and Rescue. He identifies himself, and confirms that he is indeed speaking to Jennifer, before he reveals the purpose of his call. Calloused because he has made this call several times before, governed by restraint, he simply says, "I don't want you to be alarmed. We never received a confirmation signal from your dad yesterday acknowledging his safe arrival at the Cody Landing cabin. We will begin a search and rescue mission within the hour. Please keep your phone close. I will update you as soon as we have located him. That's all I can tell you at this point." Before she is able to process what she has just been told, the call is abruptly ended and her phone is silent.

Jolted with terror by the words of Captain Dawson, she lunges out of bed in a fit of rage. Screaming, "NO! GOD! You took my mom! You took my brother! Don't do this!" Struggling to breathe, instinctively she calls Todd. Through the tears, and gasps for breath, she mutters, "He's dead. I .... uh, uh, uh, can't ... uh, uh, uh, breathe."

Todd is my closet friend. He is closer than a brother. Together we led a small group bible study for the past fifteen years. We have been there for each other through the good and the bad. The Thanksgiving holiday before Debbie died, Todd and his wife Lindsee invited us to share the Thanksgiving meal with them and their family. The night of Jason's accident, Todd was the first person that I called and asked to pray. He prayed without ceasing, all through the night; he was there to hold us up the following morning at breakfast. Todd hands the phone to his wife Lindsee. He says, "Talk to Jennifer. Keep her on the phone. Try to calm her down. I'm going to take your phone. I'm not sure what is going on, just pray for her. I have to go."

As he is pulling out of his driveway, Todd dials 911 to report a possible homicide at 607 W Carrol Street. Hoping that she can tell him what to expect before he arrives at Jennifer's house, Todd attempts to get Lindsee on the phone. The line is busy, she must still be talking to Jennifer. Fearing the worst, but straining for a glimmer of hope, as he weaves in and out of traffic, navigating across town like a Nascar driver; Todd sends a text message to Lindsee, asking what's going on. Lindsee replies in all caps; HURRY. STILL TALKING. IT'S BAD. Todd arrives to find Jennifer sitting on the floor in the corner with Jax and Jaslynn. Her breathing is like someone fighting for every breath. The look in her eyes is cold and distant. She is holding Jax and Jaslynn like a momma bear protecting her cubs. The fear on the faces of Jax and Jaslynn, because they don't have a clue as to what is going on, intensifies the chaos and confusion. As Todd kneels down to try and comfort Jennifer and the kids, police officer's storm into the room, escalating the situation to a state of complete pandemonium.

Like fighting fire with gasoline, more sirens and flashing lights as the EMT's arrive, add tension to an already bizarre scene, stressing the fabric of sanity to the point of spontaneous combustion. A female officer attempts to comfort Jax and Jaslynn. The EMT's try to calm Jennifer and regulate her breathing, while another officer seems to be attacking her with a barrage of questions about her dad. Where is he? Has he been shot? Has he fallen? Is he in the house? Are there still intruders. Where's the body? With her heart racing, and struggling to breathe, wailing uncontrollably, Jennifer attempts to explain the phone call that she received from Captain Dawson. Once the officers at the scene are able to confirm Jennifer's story, realizing that no crime has been committed, they head back to the station. The EMT's remain until Jennifer has calmed down, her blood pressure has returned to normal, and she is able to breathe without oxygen. Once the situation is diffused, and a sliver of calm returns, Todd calls Lindsee. He asks her to come and get Jax and Jaslynn, while he attempts to comfort Jennifer, and help her to figure out what she needs to do next.

As Todd sets there holding my little girl, Jennifer reaches for her phone to post a message on her Facebook page. *My daddy is missing. Please pray!* The response to Jennifer's post is immediate and overwhelming. Her phone is blowing up with private messages, text messages, and ringing constantly with incoming calls. Within the hour, two of my closest running friends, Jeff and Bryan are sitting with Todd and Jennifer. They have booked a flight to Wyoming in order to help with the search and rescue. At 11:54 AM the phone rings again. It's been ringing all morning, but this call is different. It is the same number that called at 4:00 AM. Jennifer begins to tremble and shake her head. Fearing the worst, she hands the phone to Todd.

He answers, "This is Todd Wright. I am a friend of the family. Jennifer is right here. She handed me the phone. Please tell us something good." Todd held her hand and looked straight into her eyes as he listened to the voice on the other end, trying not to show emotion if the news was bad. As he listened, his grip tightened and Jennifer began to cry. Trying to reassure her, Todd tells Jennifer that the search and rescue team found my water bottle and some blood on a technical portion of the trail. They haven't found me yet. They are hopeful that my injuries are not severe. It appears that maybe I was able to keep moving. They will keep us informed. That was all he said.

Jennifer could tell that Todd was holding back something. Deep in her soul she knew there was more he wasn't telling. This was the same feeling, she had the night, she received the call that Jason had been in a serious accident. This was the same weight pressing down on her, the day her mother died. She looked at Todd and said, "I need some air. Will you go outside with me?" As soon as they were outside, she said, "Tell me the truth. Please."

Todd said, "Your dad is a strong man. We have to believe that he is going to make it. Captain Dawson said that there was a lot of blood. From the amount of blood, it would appear that your dad's injuries may be serious. They have not found him, and there is no blood trail leading away from the accident sight. They are thinking that maybe he was able to stop the bleeding, but they are concerned that he may be disoriented and no longer following the trail. They will continue to search along the trail in both directions today. If they do not find him, they will broaden the search tomorrow and go off trail."

Her anger erupted like a volcano spewing fire and brimstone throughout the usually docile neighborhood. Feeling betrayed and abandoned, she began cursing God and shouting vulgarities like a soldier, wounded and alone, left behind enemy lines.

Later that night, as Jennifer put the kids down for bed, she says, "We need to pray for Dandy."

Jaslynn prays, "Dear Jesus, please let Nana Debbie find Dandy and help him. Amen."

Jax prays, "Dear Jesus, please let Dandy walk out of the mountains and be okay. Amen."

Jennifer kisses them both goodnight and smiles as she turns off the light, hiding her true emotions. If ever there was a time that these children needed to pray a passionate, fervent prayer, it was now. Part of her wanted to storm right back into that room. Jerk them up out of bed, shake the crap out of them, and say, "This is serious! I've lost my mom. I've lost my brother. I cannot lose my dad." How could they both offer prayers that seemed to imply that they were not worried? "God forgive them", she said. They were just children. They could not possibly understand the gravity of this situation.

They have never known the pain of losing a mother and a brother. With her head in her hands, she prays they never will, and cries out, "Thank you, Jesus that they don't have a clue."

We were all together when Debbie died. We gathered around her bed, and watched as her breathing became more faint and shallow. Her best friend was in the room, along with her nurse. Her two sisters were there also. Jennifer laid beside her. I held her hand and kissed her forehead. Jason and Adam were rubbing her feet as she took her final breath. She didn't die alone. I remember the night Jason died, Jennifer and Adam's world was turned upside down.

The night of Jason's accident, we received the call that he had been airlifted to the Trauma Treatment Center in Memphis, Tennessee. We drove an hour and a half, not knowing the extent of his injuries. Adam arrived about ten minutes before Jennifer and I did. He was setting in the parking lot, wailing as Jennifer and I drove up. He informed us that his brother's body had already been transported to the morgue. Jason died alone, with no one there to hold his hand or comfort him as he departed. Like bookends pressing in from both sides of her head, images of Jason's death and images of my death are tormenting Jennifer. Cries for help, but no one to hear. Where was God, and why would He do this again?

Exhausted but unable to sleep, disturbed by the

images haunting her every time she closed her eyes, Jennifer and Adam set up until 4:00 the next morning hoping that maybe there would be another call saying, "We've found your dad. He is a little shaken up, but he is going to be okay." There was no phone call, just a lot of tears, very little conversation, and two pots of coffee. With the walls closing in, and hope fading away like a vapor in the wind, Jennifer cries out in desperation for Jason to save her.

With no words, Adam tries to offer hope in this chasm of despair, by holding her a little tighter.

Sinking deeper into the crevasse of couch that won't let go, Jennifer cries out again. This time she pleas for me to rescue her. Shackled together, and tethered to an anchor pulling them under, as they fight for air, neither of them sees a way of escape. Jennifer reaches for a bottle of pills. She just wants the pain to go away. She has seen it before. The medicine that cures, becomes the poison that kills.

As she begins to dance with the devil, the music is interrupted by a text from Captain Dawson. It said, "Hang in there. We will broaden our search area today. We will go off trail. I will update you later this morning." Realizing how close she came to surrendering to the pain, Jennifer gets up and goes outside. The tears begin to flow. Within minutes Jaslynn comes outside smiling and says, "What's wrong mommy? Are you okay?"

Jennifer motioned for Jase to come and sit with

her. With tears unhindered and flowing freely, she holds her little girl close to her heart, and chokes on the words, "My heart hurts Jaslynn. I'm just worried about my daddy."

With a twinkle in her eye like it was Christmas morning, Jaslynn says, "Tell your heart not to hurt mommy. He's okay."

Jennifer cried all the more, torn between reality and the desire to embrace a child-like faith that has no comprehension of the word impossible. She wanted to believe. With all her heart, she wanted to believe that her daddy was going to be okay. She wanted the faith of her little girl.

Jaslynn said, "Dandy fell and he was hurt really bad. He broke his leg and his head was split open. There was a lot of blood. But Nana Debbie found him. She fixed his leg and the hole in his head. I helped Nana Debbie take care of him. I don't think Dandy knew that I was there though. I slept in a chair that night and Nana Debbie slept beside Dandy. The next morning, he was better, so Nana Debbie said that we had to go. She said Pa was going to help Dandy walk to another cabin. Pa is Dandy's dad. Did you know that?" Jennifer smiles and nods her head yes. "But Pa and Dandy aren't walking where the rescue people are looking for him. They are going in a different direction. They are going to a cabin that is about one-hundred miles south of where the searchers are looking. It's near a little creek with a waterfall that has three pools, and there is a tree that the old-timers called the *Tree of Life* because it has a heart. You need to tell the searches where to look. The place where Dandy is going, is called the portal."

Immediately, Jennifer calls Mountain Patrol Search and Rescue and asks to be patched through to Captain Dawson. She says to Captain Dawson, "This may sound crazy, but I believe that you are searching for my dad in the wrong place. My daughter had a dream last night. She said that my dad is about one-hundred miles south of where you are searching in an area called the portal."

With the same calloused tone as before, Captain Dawson replies, "Mrs. Ring, I appreciate you interest in helping us to locate your dad. I'm sure you believe that your daughter's dream is relevant. My team knows these mountains. We've performed over one-hundred successful rescue missions in the last ten years. Sixty-seven times the individual we were searching for was found alive. Time is of the essence. If we are to find your dad alive, we need to concentrate our efforts in the area where he is most likely to be found. I'm sorry, but it would be irresponsible of me to pull team members and resources and reallocate them to an area with a very low probability of finding your father. If your father is alive, and I hope he is, he has sustained severe and serious injuries. Trust me when I tell you that he has not somehow magically walked one-hundred miles to the south. Please know that I have allocated all of our resources where I believe we have the best possible chance of finding you dad. Let me do my job, and I will call you as soon as I have good news to share."

Frustrated and angry, Jennifer realizes that she has no choice, except to go to Wyoming, and personally implore Captain Dawson to redirect his search efforts. By 5:30 PM she is landing at the Jackson, Wyoming Airport. She rents a car and drives to the Mountain Patrol Search and Rescue headquarters. Charging through the front door, she marches right up to the dispatch operator and screams, "My name is Jennifer Ring and I need to see Captain Dawson right now!"

Before the dispatch operator is able to respond, a door off to her left opens. Out walks a rugged looking man, a mountain man to be sure. He said, "My name is Dawson. Please come in." In his office was a round table with two chairs. The wall was covered with maps. There was a coffee pot in the corner. He poured two cups of coffee. He said, "Let's sit, and talk." He didn't say another word. For thirty minutes he listened to Jennifer tell why she believed that he was searching in the wrong place. With empathy in his eyes, he said, "It's too late to redirect our search efforts this evening. Please give me one more day. If we don't find your dad tomorrow, then I will reassess our efforts and make a decision on Sunday as to what course of action we need to consider next week."

The next morning, convinced that Jaslynn's dream must be true, Jennifer decides to set out on her own. If Captain Dawson won't look to the south, she will search for me all by herself. She asks the lodge owner, Mr. Tackett, if he knew where there was a cabin about one-hundred miles south of town. She told him the cabin was near a tree with a heart shaped growth on the trunk, and both were located near a town called Portal.

I'm certain that Mr. Tackett thought this country bumpkin from Arkansas, had wandered out west and lost her way. He had lived in the area all of his life. The lodge had been in his family ever since the town existed. His daddy before him, and his grandpa before him, had lived in these mountains their entire lives, but he had no idea of the area she was describing. The only road that went due south out of town was Highway 14. It was a dangerous road with steep hills and hairpin curves. There was an accident sixteen years ago on a bridge about one-hundred-fifty miles south of town. Two families crashed into each other on Devil's Bridge, a one lane bridge over Sulphur Lake. Very few people lived along Highway 14 and it was several days before the accident was discovered. A young man on a motor-cycle was traveling north from Jasper and came up on the accident. He reached the bridge and was barely able to stop his bike in time. All he could see was that there had been a fire and most of the bridge was gone. An investigation revealed two vehicles in the lake. Bodies inside were badly burned and it was determined the crash must have caused an explosion of one or both vehicles killing everyone instantly. Fire destroyed the bridge and sent both vehicles plummeting into the lake below. To this date the bridge has never been repaired. The new highway intersects Highway 35 just west of Jasper. There is really nothing south of town along Highway 14, except Sulphur Lake, and no way to get across.

None of that mattered to Jennifer. She was convinced that Jaslynn's dream was real. She was determined to search every inch of Highway 14 if that was what it took to find her daddy. She filled the rental car with gas and headed south, looking for a sign, determined not to give up until she found me. The road was not for the faint of heart. At times, she drove with a death grip on the steering wheel, never getting over thirty-five miles-per-hour. It was noon, she had been driving for five hours. She had come to the end of the road. There it was, Devil's Bridge, or what was left of it. She could see charred timbers on both sides of the lake. With over one hundred feet of bridge missing, the explosion and fire must have been massive. She had come all this way, but she never saw a sign. She didn't see a tree with a heart shaped trunk. Part of her wanted to put the pedal to the metal, race forward, headlong over a bridge that wasn't there, and stop the pain. Standing at the edge of the bridge, she saw the *Angel of Death* extending an invitation. He would ease her pain, if she would surrender to the temptation. She could be set free, all she had to do was to give up, and give in. He would end it all for her right there. She could hear the music begin to play again, and part of her wanted to dance. But deep down, she still believed in Jaslynn's dream.

Reluctantly, she turned the car around and headed back north, chanting over and over in her head, "Not today Satan. Not today." Determined not to give up, she searched more intently every inch of road, as she drove back toward town, but the thread of hope that she held on to, began to unravel and give way to despair. Surely, she must have overlooked the obvious. Her mind played tricks on her. She saw things that weren't there. She heard things that weren't there. Searching the road, looking for clues, screaming at God. Cursing God, and asking, why? Where is he? Where is my daddy? Help me! Please.

Defeated, exhausted, and full of anger she finds herself back at the lodge. Believing that I was out there somewhere, she could not lock herself in her room for the night, with the walls closing in, and the bed sucking her deep into the pit of despair, where the Devil waited to Tango. She decided to wait in the café, hoping for a miracle. Hungry, but not wanting to eat, she sits in the corner, praying and cursing God. Unaware of the older man in the booth beside her, she begins to cry.

With a voice as smooth as Irish whiskey, he says, "What's a pretty little girl like you doing in a place like this, crying all alone?"

She wipes her eyes, and blows her nose, and through the tears she tells him her story. His clothes are torn. His eyes are kind and his smile reminds her of Jason's.

He says, "I know the place you're talking about. My dad used to take me there when I was a small boy. My brother and I loved that place. It's magical, you know. The cabin, you're looking for, sits back off the highway about a quarter mile. If you don't know where to look, you will never find it. I can take you there if you like. I'll take you to your dad."

A whirlwind of emotions are swirling in her head. He looks like a harmless old man, but is he what he appears to be? This old man could be Satan incarnate, attempting to lure her back to Devil's Bridge. Like a warning sign, the music begins to play softly in the background. Fear convinces her that if she doesn't dance, she will never know, if he was the sign she had been searching for.

He said, "I'll bet your daughter Jaslynn looks just like you."

The music playing softly in the back of her head, beckoning her to dance, morphed into an eerie melody that signaled something ominous was about to happen. She could not remember if she had mentioned Jaslynn by name or if she had said that her daughter had a dream. Her heart was pounding in her chest like a bass drum in a subway tunnel. Realizing that she hadn't slept in two days, she'd been driving up and down Highway 14 all day long, something told her that this old man was not who she thought he was. Looking for a way out, she said, "Let me fill the car with gas, and we'll go."

Before she could free herself from this trap she had stepped into, He said, "We can take my truck. I've got a full tank of gas, and besides, I know where we're going. Come on pretty girl. Let's go get your dad."

Distraught that this may be her only hope of seeing her daddy again, she chose to ignore the warning signs, and silenced the alarms compelling her to run. Before she realized it, she was in his truck, and they were headed toward Devils Bridge. She didn't even know his name. No one knew she had left town with this stranger. She was about to dance with the Devil in the dark.

"By the way, my name is Bill, but everyone calls me Bud." He drove down the road like he had driven it one hundred times before. Not recklessly or dangerously, but as if he knew every turn like he knew the back of his hand. The truck seemed to glide as if it were on rails.

It didn't matter if she knew who he was or not.

His name didn't change what was about to happen. Instinctively, she reached for her phone. Like the two cars colliding in the dark on Devil's Bridge, she realized that she had left her phone in the rental car. She had no phone, no weapon, and no way to defend herself.

As the eerie melody begins to play again, indicating the dance is about to commence, Bill slows his truck to a crawl. He says we are almost here. Stopping the truck in the middle of the road, he says, "There is a flashlight in the glove box, could you hand it to me?"

Jennifer reaches in the glove box. There is a hammer and a flashlight. The sight of the hammer bludgeoned the fragile veneer of hope she had been hiding behind. Trembling, she hands the flashlight to Bill. He shines it on a tree alongside the road. Could this be the sign she had been looking for? Had she missed the obvious?

Bill said, "My daddy used to tell me this was the tree of good and evil."

Through the light beam of the flashlight, Jennifer could see her breath. There was a chill in the air she hadn't noticed before. The hair on the back of her neck stood up.

Bill chuckled and said, "I'm just messing with you, pretty girl." He shined the light a little further up the tree. "Do you see that," he said. "What's that look like to you?"

There it was. A heart shaped growth about thirty foot up the trunk of the tree.

"What my daddy really told me is that this was the *Tree of Life*." And with that, Bill pulled his truck off the highway down a little lane that was completely obscured by the vegetation. He had traveled no more than one-hundred yards when he said, "We'll have to walk from here."

Jennifer got out of the truck first. She noticed that Bill reached under his seat and grabbed something before he got out. It was a machete. She couldn't move. The lump in her throat felt like a grapefruit. She couldn't scream. She wanted to run, but where would she go. Bill never looked back. He was wielding that machete with the precision of a craftsman, clearing a path in front of his truck. He had obviously been here before. Twenty yards out in front of his truck, Bill got down on his hands and knees and crawled into a crevice, or a cave, a hole or something. She wasn't sure, but she could see the light shining on the inside. He yelled back to her, "You'll have to crawl to get on this side."

A voice inside her head said, "Run!" She couldn't remember if Bill had taken the keys, or if he had left them in the truck. She wrestled with the voice of reason telling her to flee. She had come this far. She had no intentions of going back now. She got down on her hands and knees and followed Bill. He was standing up, on the other side, shining the light for her to see. Like lovers dancing in the dark, guided by the light, she followed her demon, who carried a machete down another path.

Bill said, "It's not much further now." They were walking on a trail that appeared to be maintained and well kept. Another one-hundred yards and Bill said, "We have to cross this bridge to get to the cabin." It was an old wooden bridge suspended by ropes with some of the boards missing. Bill crossed over first and shined the light back for Jennifer to cross. One missed step would be certain death. Frozen with fear, Jennifer couldn't move. Bill came back across the bridge. Jennifer's eyes were focused on the machete in Bill's hand. He says, "Climb on my back. I'll carry you across."

She knew this was a test. Something lay hidden in the woods just beyond the bridge. It was time to dance. Fear and faith, unwitting partners, had brought her to this bridge where she must choose. Death was waiting on the other side. In life or death, she believed that she would see her daddy once again. With absolute abandon, she climbed up on his back and closed her eyes.

As soon as they reached the other side, Bill put her down. Completely out of breath, he said, "It's just a little farther, but let me sit here and rest for a minute. As soon as I catch my breath we will go on." Jennifer sat on the ground. Bill laid down underneath a tree and rested his head on a stone that looked as if it had been placed there for a purpose. Something wasn't right, she could feel it. The silence was overwhelming. All she heard was the beat of her own heart and the wind blowing through the tree tops above. The music began to play again.

Instantly a thunderous crash penetrated the darkness. Bill gasped. Jennifer looked and a massive tree limb had fallen across Bill's chest. He was struggling to breathe. She attempted to lift the limb off his chest, but it was too heavy. He grabbed her hand, and said, "I'm going to be okay. Follow this trail another one-hundred yards and you will come into an opening. You will see a cabin. Dad is there."

She made one more attempt to lift the limb off his chest and set Bill free. This time she was successful. Blinded by the light, she never saw the angel standing beside her, lifting the limb. With his final breath, he says, "I love you sis." And, he was gone.

Tears rolled down her face. She leaned over and kissed his forehead. Running down the trail, with tears falling to the ground, screaming, "Daddy! Daddy, where are you?" There it was. She saw the cabin, and the door was open.

7

TO STOP THE WIND

O nce we reach the clearing where the cabin is, Jax sees Jason and takes off running. Debbie sees Jennifer and Jaslynn, and she starts running toward them. I am watching from a distance, with tears rolling down my face, but I can't move, and I can't speak. Jennifer looks back, and says, "Daddy. Daddy, come on." It's like I'm not even there. I look down. The ground is covered with blood. My leg is broken; it's no wonder that I can't move. I put my hand to my head. I feel the split in my skull, blood runs down my arm, and drips to the ground. I don't feel any pain. In fact, I don't feel anything. I see everything, in vivid detail and with great clarity. This must be Hell. Everything I love, is dancing right in front of me, but I can't touch it. I'm being restrained, and I don't know why. At that moment, Debbie looks directly at me. I'm not sure if she is looking at me, or if she is looking right through me. She smiled, and it took my breath away. Time stood still. Everything else faded away, as she began to walk toward me. Unable to move, I stand there and watch as she fades away like everything else.

Standing at the edge of a precipice, staring into the abyss, a gentle breeze caressing my face. From behind, I hear a familiar voice. I am restrained from falling this time by a firm and loving hand upon my shoulder, but no one is there. The voice says, "For this reason a man will leave his father and mother and be united to his wife, and they will become one flesh. Therefore, what I have joined together, it will never be separated. Neither death nor life, neither angels nor demons, neither the present nor the future, nor any powers, neither height nor depth, nor anything else in all creation will be able to separate the love that God the Father has blessed through Christ Jesus the Son, our Lord and our Redeemer." Everything I love, is right in front of me again. As I start to run to her, He says, "Wait. If you cross over, there is no going back. And it's not your time yet."

Bridled by confusion, I can see my dad, Jason and Jax, Jennifer and Jaslynn and Debbie. Adam and Grace with Mom Mom and Dad Dad, they're all laughing, embracing, and inter-acting with each other. Reacting impetuously, I reach for my sword of frustration and anger, prepared to do battle, I turn and demand to know why I'm not invited. I have already been there and I have come back. Tell me, who is this that wields the power to deny my presence at the table where I have already set? I can't do this alone. I will not go back without them.

The voice of compassion, stood firm in my face and rebuked my attack with a whisper of love. "Walk with Me", He said. "What you see is real. It is all real, except to Jaslynn and Jennifer and Jax this will all seem like a dream. Jaslynn is a special little girl. Let's just say that she has been chosen, but we will talk more about that later. For Debbie, and Jason, and your dad and the others, this is a special time. It is as real for them, as Me and you being here right now." With that, I turned my head and saw a man walking beside me. I had questions, but I could not speak. He said, "I know that you've got questions. There are some deep theological issues that you just can't reconcile or resolve. How about we save those for later. Let's start with what you really want to know." He stood in front of me, and showed me everything that I ever wanted to see. He showed me His hands. Broken, and poured out, I still could not speak. I had seen the love in His eyes, now I could see my name written on the palm of His hand. It was just a scar, but in the scar I saw my name written in blood, on the palm of His hand. He said, "Let's walk some more. We can start with an easy question. Every night, before you pray, you look at a picture of Debbie beside your bed. You always say, 'I love you babe, and I miss you.' Sometimes you close your eyes and you remember her smile, and those big brown eyes. You wonder if she still loves you. You wonder if she misses you. What you really want to know, is she waiting for you. Some nights you would give everything you own just to hold her, and have one more goodnight kiss. Every night I see the way that your love for her shines on, like a candle in the rain, and I smile. It is like the love I have for you, My son. It is an unyielding, and never-ending love.

Then, after you have lamented the bond of eternal love, I see something that you never see. Every night, she smiles, and says, 'I love you more.' Some nights she sits there all night and watches while you sleep. When everything else is lost, My son; faith, hope and love will remain. Don't ever forget, the greatest of these is love." Tears were rolling down my face. I had no words. I still could not speak.

"Do you remember your first race after she died? It was hot and humid that day. The temperature was near ninety degrees at the beginning of the race. You wore a white running shirt with her picture on the back. Underneath her picture, you had the words printed, *Can you see me now*? I was there that day. I ran behind you most of the race. You didn't even notice Me, until you cramped up at mile fifteen. I stopped and offered you some water. We walked together a short distance before you took off again. I stayed behind you for the rest of the race."

As He was speaking, my mind went back to that day. I knew that I had seen Him somewhere before. I said, "My bib had my name on it, DAN. My bib number was 315. Yours was 316, but it didn't have your name. It just had the initials, JC. I remembered thinking, the initials JC would fit if you were from Arkansas, but you didn't look like you were from Arkansas."

"You never noticed, but she was there too. She saw you. She didn't run, but she saw every step that you took. She was there when you crossed the finish line. She was in the crowd. And she was smiling, like I had never seen her smile before. She was so proud of you that day! Every race that you've ever run, she has been there. I have been there Myself, at every race, even when you couldn't see Me, or feel My presence. I've been there with her, encouraging you, singing over you, and we have celebrated in dance every finish line you crossed.

She was there when Jax was born, and Jaslynn and Grace. She was there when Jason died. The first responders were working frantically to free him, they had no idea of the extent of his internal injuries.

She was sitting next to him. She saw what the first responders were unable to see. Once the pressure on his chest was released, death would be instantaneous. She whispered in his ear, 'We need to get out of here.' She had been there the whole time, but he hadn't seen her until she spoke to him. He looked at her as if she was joking and said, 'I'm kind of stuck here.'

The first responder thought that Jason was talking to him. He replied to Jason, "We've almost got you free."

With that Debbie said something to Jason that he had said to her a hundred times before. She said, 'Come on baby tomato, catch up.' He smiled just as the first responders removed the steering wheel from his chest. They never knew what made him smile. And like the day she held him for the very first time, she held him again. She cried, but they were tears of joy. She smiled, and she didn't let go. You cried, and it broke My heart. I felt your pain, but there was a celebration in My Daddy's house that day! She was the woman you spoke with in the cemetery. She was the one who took care of you when you fell on the trail."

As He talked, I was able to see the things that I had never seen before. She placed a blanket on me, one winter night, after I cried myself to sleep. She laid down beside me, and kept me warm. She was the little girl on the trail that showed me a rock, and told me about Jesus. She was the stranger that stopped one day on the side of the road and offered me a bottle of water, and said, "Keep running. People are watching. You're making a difference." I see her; I see my dad and Jason; I see all the times they have been there when I thought I was alone. I see a great cloud of witnesses celebrating every victory, and every time He was there. He was there dancing and singing over me.

He said, "Now, let's get real. When Cain killed Abel, Eve asked why. Joseph asked Me why, when his brothers sold him into slavery. He asked Me why, when he was thrown into prison. I never answered Eve; I never answered Joseph. Joseph came to realize that what Satan had intended for evil toward him, I would use for good. Job asked why. John the Baptist asked why. He wanted to know if I would set him free. Every one of the disciples asked why. More than once Paul asked why. The answer is always the same. I am not the author of evil. I do not orchestrate pain, or disease, or hatred. You believe that I could have healed Debbie, but you want to know why I didn't. You believe that I could have prevented Jason's accident, and you want to know why I didn't. Tell Me, if you can, where the wind comes from or what it is made of. Describe its shape and color. Tell Me how to order its ways.

Where were you when I stretched out the mountains? Where were you when I made the wind? Do you know My thoughts? Can you turn the rising sun into darkness? Are you able to walk above the heavens, like Me? I'm not looking for answers, My son. I'm telling you what you already know. The answers you're searching for are in My Word.

I made the wind. In the book of Amos, I AM the Lord of Host. I formed the mountains and I created the wind. I declare what I will make known to man. I turn the rising sun into darkness. I walk above the heavens. I AM the Lord God Almighty!

But I do not order its ways. In the gospel of John, I made it clear that the wind blows wherever it pleases. You may hear its sound, but you cannot tell where it comes from or where it is going.

Sometimes, I stop the wind. In the gospel of Mark, I spoke to the wind. The disciples said, 'Teacher, do you not care that we are perishing?' I rose up, rebuked the wind and said to the waves, Quiet! Be still! Then the wind died down and it was completely calm.

Sometimes, I don't stop the wind from blowing. In the book of Job, Satan was permitted to use the wind to destroy Job's family. A messenger came and said to Job, 'Your sons and daughters were feasting and drinking wine at the oldest brother's house. Suddenly a mighty wind swept in from the desert and struck the four corners of the house. It collapsed on them and they are dead, and I am the only one who has escaped to tell you!'

Like Job, and Joseph, the disciples, My cousin John, and Saul of Tarsus, you do not understand what I am doing right now. But trust Me, one day you will. Until then, remember this story.

There was a man walking in the woods one day. He was a righteous man. He loved his wife. He had three beautiful girls, whom he also loved very much. His youngest daughter was seventeen, his oldest daughter was thirty-two, and the middle daughter was twenty-five. His two oldest daughters were married and had children of their own. He was an honest man and a hardworking man. He did not possess much worldly wealth, but he was richly blessed, and always willing to share with those who had less. With the sun in his face, and the wind at his back, he was giving thanks, for all that he had, as he walked. Satan caused a strong wind to blow a dead limb from the tree above the man's head. It fell across the man's neck, knocking the man to the ground. Unable to move his legs, the man crawled over a mile, back to his home. His injuries were serious, he was paralyzed from the waist down.

The man was no longer able to work his farm, he could no longer provide for his family. Because the man lived far from the doctors, who would treat him for the rest of his life, he moved his family from the home he had built with his own two hands. They purchased a small house in town, close to the store and near his doctors. His wife, who had never worked outside of the home, would now become her husband's caregiver for the rest of his life. The financial strain was difficult at times. The small country church, where he had served most of his life, was thirty miles away. The small congregation offered little help to the man and his family. The man never lost faith in God's goodness or His provision.

His youngest daughter was the most beautiful of his three girls. She was a daddy's girl. She looked like her mother. She had had brown hair, big brown eyes and a beautiful smile, but she had her father's complexion. He was part Cherokee, and she looked like an Indian princess. The accident happened her senior year in high school. Even though the family had moved thirty miles from the town which she had grown up in, she would drive to the school that she had attended all her life, so that she could graduate with her friends. Some days she would curse God as she drove to school. Some days she would pray for forgiveness and ask God to heal her daddy. Some days she would question if she was to blame for her father's tragedy.

The man himself asked God why this had happened. God never answered the man, his wife or his daughters. Two months before his youngest daughter graduated from high school, another man's house in town burned down. The second man had to move his family also. This caused the second man's son to have to drive a long distance in the opposite direction every day to work. Every day, going in opposite directions, the first man's daughter, and the second man's son would meet on the road as she was driving home from school and he was driving home from work. The second man's son was determined to meet this beautiful young girl that he was crossing paths with every day as a result of his family's recent move. One day he was telling a friend about the beautiful young girl he hoped to meet. His friend worked at a local grocery store. He often bagged groceries for the young girl. After carrying the groceries to her car, he would watch as she drove off. Her family lived less than a quarter-mile form the store's parking lot. He offered to take his friend to meet her, even though he didn't even know her name. He just knew where she lived. The first man's youngest daughter, and the second man's son met one Sunday afternoon. In less than a year, the two of them were married. They had three beautiful children. Their daughter has a beautiful little girl. She is a very special little girl.

God never answered the man, his wife or his daughters as to why this had happened."

He stopped walking. He stood still and all of creation obeyed. Time stood still. He looked square into my eyes, and asked, "Do you think I should have stopped the wind from blowing that day? Should I have stopped the limb from falling?"

Tears rolled down my face. He was telling my

story. The first man was my father-in-law. His beautiful young daughter was my wife.

He said, "Sit here with me for a while." We were back where we had started. In the distance I could see Debbie, Jaslynn, Jennifer, and Jason, Jax, my dad, and Debbie's parents along with many others.

"Do you know who those others are", He asked. Then He reminded me of something Jennifer had said to me recently. She knew that it had been a tough day for me, it had been a tough day for her as well. She was angry and sad that her mom had died. She was bitter that Jason had died. Trying to paint a silver lining around the clouds of despair, she said, "I don't think you realize, daddy, how many people you have touched; and none of it would have happened if mom and Jason were still here."

He called each one by name and told me the story of how I had impacted their lives. He said that one day each one of them was looking forward to hugging my neck and thanking me for sharing my story with them. After He told me each story, He began to tell me the stories of the people, still living on earth, whose life I had impacted. Then He told me how those that I had impacted, were impacting the lives of others.

He smiled as He told me about a young doctor, who is a gifted pediatric surgeon that has saved the lives of several small children. His name is Dr. Corey Tillman. He was a home health-care nurse that cared for Debbie during the final months of her life. This young man had become jaded and discouraged, during the short time he had spent caring for terminally ill, and elderly patients. He wanted answers. He wanted to know where God was, when his patients were suffering and dying. His older sister had died from an inoperable brain tumor. She was only thirty-four years old. She left behind two small children and a loving husband. The young hospice care nurse, who blamed God for the dying patients He could not save, was about to give up on medicine, and he was ready to give up on God. The day he met Debbie, she smiled at him, and that changed his life. He had read her chart. He knew her prognosis, but she had something his other patients didn't. In the face of insurmountable mountains, she had faith in a God who moved mountains. As cancer sucked the very breath from her lungs, she had hope in the Spirit of the Wind to raise her up, proclaiming good news and lifting the weight off those who were oppressed. In the Valley of Death, she would sit with the Shepherd, at peace in the presence of her enemy, and delight in His company. He was moved by her faith, and overwhelmed by her hope, but it was her love that he could not deny. She encouraged him to pursue a career in medicine, because he was making a difference. She made him believe that he was important to her. It was the way she lived, in the face of death that opened his eyes to a light of hope shining bright in the darkness.

He said, "You don't realize it, but this gifted pediatric surgeon looks up to you, the guy who runs up and down the highway. He watches you from a distance. In the short time that he cared for Debbie, he caught a glimpse of what you lost. To see how you have inspired others, after losing her, and then losing Jason, has given him hope."

Once more, He looked me square in the eye, and asked, "Do you think I should have stopped the wind from blowing? Should I have stopped the limb from falling?"

Before I could answer, He said, "I did not come to stop the wind. I came to pick up the broken pieces. I came to take what is broken and make something beautiful. I came to reverse the curse. I came to bless the broken road. I am telling you what I told Jeremiah. If you go to the Potter's house, you will see that the broken vessel, in the Potter's hand, becomes His treasure."

He continued by saying, "There is something else that you need to see." We watched as a young mother strapped her little girl in the car seat of her SUV. Her purse was sitting up front in the empty seat. I could see a gun and a bottle of pills beside her purse. The night was dark and stormy. The wind was howling. He told me that they were on their way to Grandma's house. The young mother, was a single mom, she was going to drop off her little girl. Then she planned to drive to a spot down by the lake, where an older man told her, that he loved her six years ago. After the man found out that she was pregnant, he told her that she should have an abortion, and that he never wanted to see her again. She plans to stop at the liquor store, after she drops her little girl off, and get a bottle of Jack Daniels. A bottle of Jack, a bottle of pills, and a loaded hand gun is how she plans to end the pain.

We watched as she drove along the dark and winding two lane road. I knew something bad was going to happen. This was the same road that Jason had his accident on. In the distance I see another car coming from the other direction. I wanted to scream out, *Do something*. That's when I realized the other car was Jason's. As they approach the curve, the young mother swerves to miss something in the road. In the blink of an eye, the two cars collide head on. She is shaken up a bit, but she is not hurt. She manages to get out of her vehicle and goes around to check on her little girl. As she approaches the rear passenger door to check on her daughter, she trips over a limb in the road. Once she realizes that her daughter is not injured, she goes to check on the other driver. She can tell the small coupe did not fare as well as her larger SUV. In fact, the front of the smaller car appears to be heavily damaged.

Jason is conscious, but unable to free himself from the wreckage. With the engine block in his lap, he has no feeling in his legs. The steering wheel is pressing down like a weight on his chest. His lungs are collapsed making his breathing arduous. She returned to her vehicle to call 911. After calling for help, she took her daughter in her arms and walked back to Jason's vehicle, to comfort him until help arrived. Standing in the presence of the Spirit of the Wind, having been acquitted by His scandalous grace, she no longer wanted to end her life. The curse of wine and ecstasy had been reversed. Holding the gift of life in her arms, she introduced her little girl to Jason, saying, "This is Aiyana, my little princess. Her name means *Endless Beauty*. She wants to pray for you, if that's okay."

Jason smiled, nodded his head, and said, "I would like that very much."

Aiyana reached out to take hold of Jason's hand. In her eyes, he saw the nail pierced hand reach out to rescue him. In that moment, he knew that he was held in the palm of her hand as she prayed.

She said, "Dear Jesus, mommy says a miracle is when something bad happens, and then God makes something beautiful happen. We're sorry Jesus that this bad accident happened. Please send an angel to help Mr. Jason, and do a miracle Jesus. Please make this bad accident turn out to be really beautiful, just like you Jesus. Amen."

Within a matter of minutes, police officers and an ambulance arrived. The call was made to the rescue squad, requesting the *Jaws of Life* in order to free Jason from his crumpled car. As the rescue squad worked to free Jason, the young mother called her mom. She told her that she and Aiyana had been in an accident, but neither of them was seriously injured. When her mother arrived, the young girl said, "A strong wind blew a dead limb from that tree into the road. I swerved to miss it. I hope the other guy is going to be okay."

Next, I see a couple kneeling at an altar in a small room crying, and praying. Confused, I ask, "Who are they?"

He says, "You don't know them. Their little girl is very sick. Her kidneys are failing. They are praying for a miracle." He shows me the room where their daughter's life, is not resting in the hands of an omnipotent God, but is dependent upon the medical technology of man. She appears almost lifeless as the doctor leaves her room and heads in the direction of the prayer room. The look of dread on his face expresses the hopelessness of the situation. As the doctor enters the prayer room, a nurse walks into the young girl's room. She takes hold of the girl's hand and whispers something to her. The young girl opens her eyes and smiles. As the nurse is leaving her room, I realize that it wasn't a nurse. It was Debbie. I assume she has told the young girl that it is about to be over, and everything is going to be okay. Surely, that is what made her smile. The doctor tells the parents that their daughter might not make through the night. He suggests that they go and spend some time with her. As they walk into their daughter's room, she smiles at them, and says, "A nurse just told me everything was going to be okay. She said that I was going to get new kidneys." Then she closed her eyes, but she was smiling.

The doctor struggled to maintain his composure as he exited the young girl's room. With indignation in his voice, he inquired at the nurse's station to find out who had talked to his patient. None of the nurses had been to her room. Jesus looked at me and said, "After she received her new kidneys, she made a complete recovery. She has told her story to over 50,000 young people about how a young man, thirty-three years old, had to die when she was sixteen years old, so that she might live. When she tells her story, she says his name was Jason. Then she says, 'Two thousand years ago another young man, thirty-three years old died so that you and I might live. His name is Jesus.'"

Next, we see a man being prepped for surgery. "Who is that?" I ask.

"His name is Phil, everyone calls him Pistol. He needs a new heart. His is damaged. He is about to receive Jason's heart."

I remember the words spoken to me by the woman in the cemetery as she stood over Jason's stone. "For a little while his light shined bright in the dark of night. You will never know this side of heaven the number of lives he has impacted. You may not see him any longer, convinced that the darkness has overcome his light, but he lives on, and his light still shines."

I stand in awe, as I consider the shattered lives, uncountable, that have been resurrected from the fallen limb. I am captivated by the beauty of intricate design, as the Master Couturier weaves a tapestry of life, from the ashes of death, and disturbs the darkness with glorious light.

"Phil beat a man to death with a pistol when he was sixteen years old. No charges were ever filed. The man was his little league coach. During the investigation, it was revealed that the man had been sexually abusing Phil for six years. One day before practice, Phil walked in and caught his coach abusing another ten-year boy. That day vengeance was acquitted, and everyone lost. Another young boy lost his innocence. The coach lost his life, and Phil lost his way. He had been dealt a bad hand from the beginning. Phil had been in the Foster Care system since he was six-years old. His mom overdosed on heroin when he was four. His dad is serving a life sentence for killing a woman in a convenience store robbery that went bad. When Phil was seventeen, he forced a young girl to have sex with his friends for money. After a party, where she had been gang raped by eight of his friends, she took her own life. A few years later, Phil became the manager of one of the largest truck-stops in Atlanta Georgia. He was involved in a global sex-trafficking operation that trafficked young girls all across America. He has done some vile and ugly things."

Filled with rage and hatred toward this man I didn't even know. I stood ready to seize the tapestry of life from the Weaver's hand. Grace be damned. Let justice be served. I cried out, "Wait! NO! Why is he getting Jason's heart?"

With compassion beyond my comprehension, He looked at me and said, "Those who have good hearts don't need new hearts. Those who are healthy don't need a physician, but those who are sick do. I did not come to rescue the righteous. I came to rescue sinners. Two years ago, Phil drove two hundred miles to a Friday night high school football game, to meet two young girls that he had planned to abduct. He had developed an online relationship with the girls under the pretense of representing a modeling agency. He lured them in with the offer of money, travel to exotic destinations for photo shoots, along with a glamorous lifestyle. The girls were waiting at the game. Each girl, had told her parents that she was staying the night with the other girl, after the game."

He must have known that I had heard all this story that wanted to hear. He directs my attention to Richard and Summer Litchken. Their seventeen-year-old daughter, Jessica, went to a Friday night football game, and never came home. One week later, as Richard was approaching his office building, a young girl stopped him and asked for money. As he fumbles in his wallet for a couple of dollars, an accomplice brushes up against him undetected, and drops a cell phone into the pocket of his coat. Before he reaches the front door, the phone begins to ring. Instinctively, assuming that it is his phone, he reaches into his coat pocket and pulls out the phone. The caller ID indicates the call is coming from his daughter. His heart begins to race as he answers the call. "Jessica. Jessica, is that you?"

Immediately, he realizes it's not his little girl. The voice on the other end is distorted but clearly understandable. "You are being watched. Listen very carefully if you want to see your daughter again. No police. No FBI. No media. Go to your office. Get to work, as if everything is normal."

Before the call is ended, he hears his daughter scream, "Daddy! Daddy!"

Richard was not accustomed to being told what to do. He managed a very successful private hedge fund. His personal net worth was in excess of fifty million dollars. As he closes his office door, he takes out his personal cell phone and calls his wife. Immediately, he receives a text on the burner phone, *Tell her nothing!*

When Summer answers, Richard says, "I forgot to tell you that I love you this morning when I left. I'm sorry. I just ..."

Summer interrupts, "It's okay. We will find her. I know we will."

As he hangs up, he receives another text on the burner phone, *You are being watched.*

As he stares at the phone, the text message disappears. There is no trace of the previous text. There is no record of the call in the call log. Over the next two weeks he continues to receive messages with instructions to wire one million dollars each day, until a total of ten million dollars has been transferred to a numbered account. He is told that once the total has been transferred, his daughter will be returned. If at any time, the media or the authorities are alerted, he will never see his daughter alive again. Each day, at work, Richard receives pictures of his daughter no father should ever see. The photos of his daughter, always disappear moments after he has seen them. They are always followed with a text, *End her pain.*

Three days after the full amount of money had been transferred, Richard continued to receive pictures of his little girl being abused. After four days with no pictures or text messages, Richard and Summer decided to contact the Federal Bureau of Investigation. They told their story, and turned the phone over to the FBI. The phone contained no history of phone calls, text messages, or pictures. A missing seventeen-year-old girl, wealthy parents, and a Russian phone with no detectable data, doesn't lend a great deal of creditability to Richard's story. With no new leads, and no hard evidence to support Richard's bizarre story, the FBI decide to call Richard and Summer back to the Bureau in order to answer questions about the phone, and to recount their story one more time.

As agent Fuentes is asking Richard to confirm, that the phone in their possession, is indeed the phone which he claimed to receive the messages and pictures on, an incoming video is received. Thirty-seven seconds of stuff no one ever wants to see. The video ends with her index finger on her right hand being cut off, and the words, *It's over!* When the phone was analyzed again, like all previous calls, texts, and pictures, there was no evidence it ever occurred. Three weeks later, Richard and Summer received a package containing an index finger. DNA confirmed it belonged to their daughter Jessica.

As another limb came crashing down, I wanted to know how the One who held the stars in His right hand could stand and do nothing to ease her pain. I turned, and saw His broken body. His blood spilled out upon the ground. Love, like a river, flowed from His eyes of compassion. Tears mingled with blood, at His feet on barren ground. Anguish crowned His brow. In His right hand, He held a double-edged sword, dripping with blood, drawn from the scales of justice. Hanging from His belt were the keys of Death and Hades. Behind the tears, burned an unquenchable, voracious fire, declaring justice.

His countenance became radiant like the rising sun, like a prisoner set free from the curse of death. His left hand held a pardon written in red. In the face of this scandalous grace, the progeny of darkness denied the light and rejected the offer. The Lamb of God sheathed His sword, and with His word He dealt the fatal blow. A beast rose up from the grave to claim the unrepentant soul.

I turned to look again, and standing in the midst of the blood and tears, was the Spirit of the Wind. Her broken body had pierced His palms, with fatal wounds, a crown of thorns upon His brow. A Roman soldier pierced His side. And when her pain was more than He could bear, heaven rejoiced as she drew her final breath. Blood flowed from Immanuel's veins. Love had crucified a rose. Yet as He hung upon that tree, He never let her go. He began to shape the broken pieces into what she had always been, a priceless treasure in His heart. By clinging to a wooden cross, He purchased with His own blood, what He already owned; and she became His pearl of greatest price.

He told me that six months later, Richard walked away from the corporate world. He and Summer bought a ranch in Montana. They established a refuge for young girls who have been rescued from sex trafficking. And just like you, they still grieve for what they lost. Through their pain, they plant seeds of hope in the fields of adversity; with blood and tears they moisten hardened ground. When the roses bloom, I come to the garden, and I sit in the midst of its beauty. The sound I hear dancing in My ear, is a melody so sweet that even the birds hush their singing. The fragrant soul of every rescued girl is a sweet aroma carried by the Spirit of the Wind. Creation rejoices in the presence of the infinite, abandoned splendor of Jehovah revealed in a single rose. And I tarry there, and the joy I share with every rose, none other, has ever known.

Thirty-seven miles outside of town, Phil stops at rest area. He does not want to risk potentially being captured on some convenience store video footage in town. As he attempts to merge back onto the highway, a gust of wind blows an empty Walmart bag, litter from an overturned garbage can, into the driver's face of an approaching vehicle. The driver swerves left, and over corrects, just clipping the front bumper of Pistol's car as it is crossing in front of him. Pistol reacts by slamming on his brakes. He is rear-ended by a third vehicle leaving the rest area also. The driver of the first vehicle, a classic 1965 Pontiac GTO convertible, veers off the right shoulder of the road, over reacting again. He loses control, doing a complete 360, veering across all four lanes of traffic. He narrowly misses being hit by and eighteen-wheeler, and a mother in a mini-van with her two small children, before coming to a complete stop on the opposite shoulder of the highway.

Neither Pistol nor the driver who struck him from the rear were severely injured. The front end of Pistol's vehicle was damaged. The headlight on the driver's side was busted. Somehow the front, driver's side tire was punctured and is flat. The impact to the rear of his car broke both tail lights. The driver of the vehicle that rear-ended Pistol was an attractive young woman. She was emotionally shaken but not physically injured, bruised from the impact of the air-bag, but she sustained no serious injuries. Within a matter of minutes, blue lights were flashing as a State Trooper, who just happened to be headed to the same football game came up on the accident. Before long, two deputy sheriffs and another State Trooper arrive on the scene. As the troopers and deputies attempt to gather information about the accident, the young woman, with tears in her eyes, apologizes to Pistol for running into the rear of his vehicle.

She had stopped at the rest area to pray. She told Pistol that she was on her way to a football game where she was supposed to speak during the opening ceremony before the game. She looked at the other driver, and then back at Pistol and said, "You and I are fortunate, but that other guy almost died." Then she said, "I almost died four years ago. I contracted a virus, on a church mission trip to Ecuador that attacked my kidneys. I was at death's door, at Children's Hospital. The doctors had said that I would not live through the night. My parents were praying for a miracle. A young man died that night in an automobile accident. I received his kidneys. His name was Jason. He wasn't much older than I am right now." She paused for a minute, then looked Pistol square in the eyes and asked, "Do you believe in miracles?" Before he could answer, she asked another question, "Do you believe in God?"

In his eyes, she saw despair, pain and loneliness. Tears began to roll down the calloused face of this hard-hearted individual. Then she said, "Another young man died two-thousand years ago. His name was Jesus. He died so that you and I might live. He died to set us free from the pain, and anger, and demons that trouble us. He died to reconcile us, to the God that loves us, with a love so scandalous, He chases us down streets no Father should ever have to walk while searching for His child." She paused again, to look into his eyes. She said, "I don't know why I'm telling you this. This is my story; this is what I was supposed to share before the game tonight. I told you that I had stopped at this rest area to pray. I prayed specifically for two things. I prayed that God would use my story tonight to reach someone that desperately needed to hear it. And I prayed something I never prayed before. I prayed that nothing bad would happen at the game tonight."

Pistol had not said a word. He continued to struggle, trying to hold back the tears. He wanted to walk away. His legs would not move. His mouth would not speak. She reached out and took hold of his hand. With compassion that he had never seen before, she said, "I want to pray for you." It wasn't her strength that held him there. It was love that would not let him go. She began to pray, asking God to rescue him. She asked for God to open his eyes to a love so deep, so scandalous, so intimate that even a prostitute could find grace at the foot of the cross. Her simple prayer was cutting to the heart of a man that had died years ago, and pouring new oil on the wounds of an innocent child.

Jesus looked at me and said, "This is why I came. I came to rescue sinners, like Phil. I came to pick up the broken pieces."

Pistol never made it to the football game that night. He no longer manages the truck stop in Atlanta. He drives a big-rig across the country now, rescuing young girls from sex trafficking and prostitution. He tells a story of love and grace, so scandalous that it rescued a wretch like him. He tells them Jessica's story. He tells them Jason's story. He tells them Jesus' story. Two years ago, he was at a truck stop in Dallas. Someone had left a flyer on the table about a couple whose daughter had been abducted at a football game by a sex trafficking organization, abused, tortured, and ultimately murdered. Their names were Richard and Summer Litchken. They would be speaking at a local church that evening, telling their story, about how God was using them to rescue other young girls. Phil knew their story. What he needed to know was just how far God's grace would reach. He went to the church that night. He listened to their story. At the conclusion of the program, he walked up to Richard and Summer, and told them who he was. He told them his story, how he had received a new heart. He told them Jessica's story, and Jason's story. Today, they work together rescuing young girls. They have rescued over three-hundred young girls, and touched the lives of hundreds more.

We walked a little farther and sat down. He said, "Let's sit here and rest for a minute before we head back to the cabin." We sat down, and He handed me a piece of fruit. We just sat there, two guys staring off into distance, eating apples. My mind drifted back to the day, Jason and I sat on his front porch eating apples.

As I gazed into eternity, I turned and asked, "What day is this?"

He said, "In this place, the sun rises and the sun sets, but the days have no number." Before I could ask what He meant by that, He said, "You need to go back now."

As I walked back to the cabin, I pondered the things He had said to me. When I got back, Jennifer, Jaslynn, and Jax were still asleep. Everyone else was gone. Exhausted, I laid down and drifted off to sleep.

8

THE GRAVE

The next thing I remember, is being startled by a loud crashing sound, and hearing Jennifer screaming, "Daddy! Daddy!" I stumble out of the cabin, half asleep. I see my little girl running toward me. Tears begin to roll down my face, but I can't move. I look down, there is a scar on my leg, but it is not broken. I rub my forehead, I feel the scar, but there is no blood. Trapped in the land of dreams, searching for the key that will set me free, I begin to question the existence of reality. I wonder, does she even see me, or is she running toward the cabin, hoping to find something that is not there. If

I'm not here, I must still be there, and she will see me unresponsive because I'm dead. I feel her breath upon my face. The beating of her heart is like the rhythmic pounding of a bass drum. With tears running down her face, she said, "Daddy, are you okay?"

I smiled, and said, "Are you real?"

She said, "I'm real daddy, and I'm here to take you home."

When she was eight years old, I took her to the park to play. She did not always see me, but I never took my eyes off of her. Running from the swings to the slide, she fell and bumped her head. Banged up a little, and confused because she didn't see me, she began to cry. I walked toward her, and stopped a few feet in front of her. I got down on my knees, and held my arms open wide, and said, "You're okay Beautiful. Come here, and let me take you home." She ran and leaped into my arms. We laughed, and we cried, and we held tight to each other like we never wanted to let go. Both of us had so much to say, but neither of us said a word. Did she indeed hold the keys to reality? Was she the bridge that would lead me home? A part of me didn't even care. There was an overwhelming sense of peace in that moment, in that place, with my little girl in my arms like she was eight years old again. I was her knight in shining armor, she was my princess, and I was here to rescue her. A time of innocence, before life had tripped us up and left us scarred and calloused. Today, she was my valiant warrior princess that had come to rescue me. There was an overwhelming awareness that we were standing on hallowed ground, in the presence of the unseen Prince of Peace. Real or not, I wasn't going to let go. I said, "I love you Beautiful."

She said, "I love you daddy. I love you so much." Neither of us wanted to let go. Neither of us wanted to leave.

With tears of joy rolling down her face, Jennifer said, "We have to go, daddy. We have to check on Bill. I'll explain everything in a minute, but Bill is hurt, and he is hurt really bad."

As she took off toward the trail, I said, "Wait. Up ahead on this trail is a bridge, just across the bridge is a crevice in some rocks that we have to crawl through, and beyond the crevice is a tree with a heart shaped growth on the trunk out by the road."

She said, "Yes daddy, but Bill is up here just this side of the bridge. He was hurt when a huge tree limb fell across his chest. I'm afraid he is dead, daddy."

As unyielding as the grave, she races to the spot where she left Bill laying on the ground. In a blaze of clarity, I am confronted with the evidence that I am running, something I haven't done since I fell on the trail. Crashing head first into a wall that wasn't there, she stopped without warning. Restrained by the unseen, she fixed her eyes upon the headstone where Bill had laid. Without a word, the stone reflected the light of the moon penetrating the tree-tops above, revealing the barren plot of ground, and declaring, "He is not here." The tree stood as a cross behind the stone. The light of love warning the weary seafarer to come no closer. With the wind and waves crashing against the shore, the fallen limb demanded a sacrifice that set me free.

For the past several days, I have wrestled with reality. Confusion and uncertainty have been my companions. But like shifting sand, the momentum has been altered, and confidence has been transferred. Jennifer appears to be confused by what she cannot see. A dead man does not get up and walk. But Bill is not there. Against all logic, she hopes that somehow, he managed to make his way back across the bridge, and down the trail. He must be waiting for us in his truck.

She does not dare to pick up his machete, but leaves it lying on the ground beside his stone. Cautiously, we crossed the bridge and followed the trail until it ended, looking for any sign that Bill had come this way. Jennifer got down on her hands and knees and said, "Follow me." We came out the other side; we could see Bill's truck sitting ahead of us on the trail, but there was no sign of Bill. Going back and searching the trail for Bill again, in the dark, would be nothing more than an exercise in futility. We were both exhausted, but neither of us wanted to leave a wounded man, alone in the woods.

We back-tracked all the way to the bridge, searching in the dark, but the woods offered no sign of Bill, and yielded no cry for help, as we called his name. We returned to the truck, and what should have been a time of celebration, was displaced by a since of guilt, as we considered heading back to town alone. I convinced Jennifer that the best hope of finding Bill, would be to send the search and rescue patrol back at first light.

Standing on the trail, beside Bill's truck, she asked me how I knew about the bridge, the crevice, and the tree, if I had not been this way before.

I said, "I don't know. I think, maybe one day, we come back here, all of us, me, you, Adam, Jax, Jaslynn, and Grace. But the part that I don't understand, I think it has already happened."

We talked non-stop all the way back to town. She told me about Jaslynn's dream, and how she had come looking for me by herself. Then she told me about meeting Bill at the café back in town, and how he brought her to where I was. She said at times, she was frightened; but there were times, she said that Bill reminded her of Jason.

I told her about falling on the trail, breaking my leg and splitting my head open. I told her there were times that I thought I was going to die, and there were times I wondered if I had died. I told her that her mom, and Jaslynn had cared for me after I fell. I told her about spending a couple days with dad.

We both knew that it would take time to understand everything that had taken place. The first thing that we needed to do, was to notify Mountain Patrol Search and Rescue that I was okay, and we needed to make certain that someone went to look for Bill. It was still dark as we pulled back in to the lodge. The moon and stars had been displaced by clouds and a dense fog that had settled all around. We parked the truck where Bill had parked it, before he and Jennifer came to look for me. Jennifer retrieved her phone from the rental car. I walked into the café and ordered coffee for the two of us. Jennifer called Captain Dawson and gave him the good news.

Within thirty minutes Captain Dawson and the local Sherriff were sitting across from us asking questions non-stop. No one remembered seeing Bill's truck sitting across the street before this morning. No one remembered seeing an old man around town the past couple of days either. Captain Dawson agrees to send a team to search for Bill. Jennifer tells them about the tree of life exactly one-hundred miles south from the spot where Bill's truck is parked. She describes the heart shaped growth about thirty feet up the trunk, the lane, the trail, the bridge, and the cabin.

Hoping to identify the owner of the truck, the sheriff runs the tags through the department of motor vehicle data base. The truck is registered to Bill Johnson. He had lived around there years ago. Everyone who knew Bill called him Bud. The owner of the café tells the story about how Bill died. He was part of a rescue team looking for a lost girl in the woods. Bill was searching alone, when he found her. She was hurt and unable to walk. He carried her across a wooden bridge, where they sat down to rest for a minute. He radioed their position to the search team coordinator. As they were talking, the dispatch operator heard a loud crash. When the rest of the team arrived, they found Bill laying on the ground with a huge limb across his chest. He was holding the little girls' hand and telling her everything would be okay. When the team lifted the huge limb off his chest, Bill gasped for breath, and he was gone.

The sheriff told us that Bill had no family except a brother who lived in Texas. He remembered that Bill's brother had taken the truck back to Texas. Possibly Bill's brother had driven the truck back to town for some reason. When the sheriff attempted to track down Bill's brother, he discovered that the brother died in an automobile accident six months earlier. His chest was crushed by the steering wheel in a head on collision. After several more cups of coffee, a hearty breakfast, and the conclusion of our informal interrogation, Jennifer and I are ready to make our way to the airport, and head home. We leave the keys to Bill's truck at the sheriff's office. Later that afternoon, the sheriff attempts to move the truck, but it won't start. When he looks under the hood, he sees that the battery is corroded, and the cables are not even connected.

In a small and neglected cemetery, at the edge of town, Jennifer and I decide to look for Bill's' grave. She wanted to place a rose on his stone. It was a simple marker, with a lighthouse etched in the stone, below the lighthouse, was this verse: "The Lord is my light and my salvation – Whom shall I fear?"

The two of us just stood there, looking at each other, and weeping. She asked if she could have a moment to herself. We were both exhausted. As I turned toward the car, I asked her if she was going to be okay. She nodded her head and said, "I'll be fine."

Looking back, I could see it all. Every year I had placed a single rose upon her stone. Today she takes the rose, and smiles at me, and lays it down with love beneath the lighthouse. The lighthouse, that stands as a beacon of hope in the dark of night as the storms of life rage all around. The beam of light, is her love that has penetrated the darkest places in my soul since she has been gone. She has always been my solid rock. Like a gentle breeze on a summer's day, I hear a voice whisper, "Behold, I have placed in Zion a stone, a tested stone, a costly stone for the foundation, firmly placed. He who believes in it will not be disturbed."

I close my eyes, for just a moment, so that I might be fully immersed in what I'm seeing. As the world begins to fade away, and I am left alone with the vision in my head, the silence is abruptly interrupted by an incoming text message on my phone.

ABOUT THE AUTHOR

Dan Ring is an avid outdoor enthusiast. He is an accomplished long-distance runner, cyclist, and tri-athlete. He is a city boy who moved down south, and fell in love with a country girl. Her name was Debbie. They had three children – Jason, Jennifer and Adam.

It was Dan's first born grandson, Jaxton that taught this longtime follower of Jesus Christ, Sunday school teacher, and deacon in the Baptist church that life is a lot more fun when you start your day with cartoons and Cocoa Puffs. Jaxton was the inspiration for Dan's first book, PRAY LIKE A CHILD.

It was his granddaughter, Jaslynn that taught him how to dream again, how to breathe again when death held ransom the very breath of life. She was the inspiration for this book.

Made in the USA
Columbia, SC
04 February 2022